Don't look back, Cristina told herself. ***This wasn't meant to be. Just keep walking.***

But she couldn't just walk away. And, really, what difference would it make if she took one last look?

She turned, and suddenly her heart was hammering louder than the rain.

Luis was still sitting there, watching her, rain running down his face.

Cristina shivered.

He was waiting.

For her.

For a moment she hesitated.

Don't—don't go back. It's just because you're nervous about tomorrow, and when you get nervous you make stupid decisions.

Her heart kicked against her ribs, and then she was walking, running back across the square, and what she was feeling wasn't nervousness but relief. And then he was pulling her against him, his mouth seeking hers, his hands sliding beneath the soaking fabric of her top.

Louise Fuller was a tomboy who hated pink and always wanted to be the prince—not the princess! Now she enjoys creating heroines who aren't pretty pushovers but are strong, believable women. Before writing for Harlequin, she studied literature and philosophy at university and then worked as a reporter at her local newspaper. She lives in Tunbridge Wells with her impossibly handsome husband, Patrick, and their six children.

Books by Louise Fuller

Harlequin Presents

Kidnapped for the Tycoon's Baby
Blackmailed Down the Aisle
Claiming His Wedding Night
A Deal Sealed by Passion
Vows Made in Secret

Visit the Author Profile page
at Harlequin.com for more titles.

Louise Fuller

———

SURRENDER TO THE
RUTHLESS BILLIONAIRE

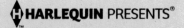
HARLEQUIN PRESENTS®

Recycling programs
for this product may
not exist in your area.

ISBN-13: 978-1-335-50436-4

Surrender to the Ruthless Billionaire

First North American publication 2018

Copyright © 2018 by Louise Fuller

Printed in U.S.A.

SURRENDER TO THE RUTHLESS BILLIONAIRE

To Millie. For always smiling. Even when I'm really annoying. And for making me laugh. Love you lots.

And to Nic. For reading, rereading, reassuring me and generally being the best editor. Thank you.

CHAPTER ONE

DOWNSHIFTING THROUGH THE GEARS, Luis Osorio slowed his vintage Ducati motorbike to a standstill and let the engine idle in neutral. As he gazed down the hill at the city illuminated in the late afternoon sunlight his heart did a *paso doble* inside his chest.

Segovia. Finally he was home.

He had deliberately left the motorway some twenty minutes earlier in order to enjoy this moment—a moment of private communion with the city of his childhood.

A city he loved.

A city he'd shunned for five years.

Five years that had felt like a life sentence.

Although really he'd got off lightly…

His breath caught in his chest and he felt a twisting rush of guilt that made his hands tighten painfully around the handlebar grips.

It was the same guilt that had almost stopped him from coming home. But this time he'd had no choice. His mother's sixtieth birthday was a celebration he couldn't miss, whatever the consequences to himself, and so he'd reluctantly agreed to fly in the morning before her party then catch a flight back to California at the weekend.

Her actual birthday was just over a week later, and he knew that his parents had been hoping he would stay. He'd wanted to, and he would have done so only—

Only that would mean forgetting the past and trying to celebrate a present none of them had ever imagined, much less wanted. There was no way he could face that. Nor could he imagine being able to keep his emotions locked down for longer than a couple of days.

It would be better—easier and less painful— to go to the party, so that was what he'd agreed with his parents.

His jaw tightened. He knew they were disappointed but he could live with that. His mouth thinned. In fact he welcomed their disappointment, for he deserved it more than they knew.

But then without telling them he'd changed his mind and instead he'd flown to Athens a month earlier than planned, bought this bike and taken the road trip across Europe that he and his brother, Bas, had promised to do together.

It was the best, the only way he could think to honour Bas's memory.

His head swam and he felt the same surge of guilt and loneliness that came whenever he thought about his brother. Bas—Baltasar—his best friend as well as his brother. And now he was gone.

On the flight over he'd told himself that it was the right time to come back, that five years of self-imposed exile would be long enough. Only now that he was here he knew that he'd been kidding himself. That nothing—no words, no gestures—could atone for what he'd done.

But he couldn't just sit there, trapped in the endless maze of his thoughts. Soon enough he was going to have to face his past—but not yet. First he wanted just one last night—not of freedom but of fantasy. A chance to cheat time...to forget who he was and what he'd done.

He breathed out slowly, listening to his heartbeat, and then, twisting the throttle, he leaned forward, feeling the bike move beneath him as he accelerated down the road.

After the wide emptiness of the motorway the city streets seemed narrow and busy. Braking gently to avoid an elderly couple crossing the road, Luis glanced up at the five-star Palacio Alfonso VI hotel. It was tempting to book a room there. Despite his dishevelled appearance, he had no doubt that the roll of banknotes in his back pocket would ensure a warm welcome.

But right now he needed more than a generous-sized bed and a power shower. He wanted anonymity. And he wouldn't get that in a hotel like the Alfonso VI.

Scooting down the side streets, he found what he was looking for twenty minutes later. This hotel only had two stars, and it was not central. But it was clean and unobtrusive, and the *dueño* was a keen biker himself. Not only did he have a lock-up for the bike, he offered to pressure-wash it too.

Two hours later, having showered and changed into his cleanest pair of jeans and a plain black T-shirt, Luis walked back out onto the street. The *dueño* had obviously kept his promise—aside from a couple of scratches to the metalwork, his bike looked just as it had when it had left the showroom and, climbing on, he set off towards the city centre.

It was warm enough for him not to need his battered leather jacket, but over the last few days he'd grown comfortable wearing it—he particularly liked the way it seemed to discourage anyone from trying to make conversation.

Although, remembering his reflection in the hotel bathroom's small mirror, it seemed unlikely that would be a problem anyway. The dark, rough stubble shadowing his jaw and the coolness in his equally dark grey eyes would probably deter all but the most persistent or thick-skinned of people from talking to him.

Outside, the light was starting to fade as he made his way through the crowds spilling off the pavements. He had no real idea of where he was going, and yet for once he didn't care. He was happy to drift through the streets for it felt so familiar—the warm night, the buzz of chatter and laughter, the smell of oranges and exhaust fumes.

It was as though the last five years had never happened. If he closed his eyes he could almost imagine that Bas was there beside him, that at any moment he would slap him round the shoulder and tell him to lighten up, because tonight was the night he would meet the woman of his dreams.

Lost in thought, he stared dazedly across the square.

As a child, the four years between them had felt vast. Then his big brother had been so much taller than him, handsome, sporty. The coolest person on the planet, in fact. Of course he'd got older and grown taller himself, until finally they were the same height. But in his head nothing had changed. Bas had always been his big brother, always at the centre of everything, his dark eyes pinballing across the room to whatever beautiful girl had caught his attention.

Whatever beautiful girl had caught his attention...

The words were still echoing inside his head

as he sidestepped carefully through the groups of people pacing the pavements like glossy thoroughbreds in a paddock when from nowhere his gaze collided with a pair of soft brown eyes the colour of *dulce de leche*.

For a fraction of a second heat—unexpected and all-consuming—burned his skin. He registered traffic-stopping red hair, a husky laugh and long golden limbs. And then, just like that, she was gone, swallowed into the crowd funnelling through the doorway into a nightclub.

He stared after her, motionless, another ripple of heat that had nothing to do with the air temperature thrumming across his skin. And then moving swiftly, he did something he'd never done before. He followed her.

Inside, the club was exactly the kind of place he loathed and normally avoided. Hot, loud and crowded, with a dress code and a VIP area. The men were sleek and groomed, the women doubly so.

But he spotted her as soon as he stepped through the door.

How could he not?

Even without the warning beacons of that striking auburn hair and those matching crimson lips, the young men congregating around her like a pack of hungry coyotes made her impossible to miss.

He gritted his teeth. It was easy to see the attraction.

Her feminine curves promised the kind of pleasure that men would fight for with their fists, and she was beautiful and confident in her charms in a way that reminded him painfully of his brother. But that was where the similarity ended, for Bas had never sought the attention he'd received, whereas this woman was deliberately using her beauty and her body to seduce.

His groin tightened as his eyes swept over her.

Okay, maybe that wasn't completely fair.

Her bright yellow top covered her arms and breasts, and her shorts were actually modest in comparison to those worn by most of the women in the club. But they still revealed an inordinate amount of long golden legs—legs that ended in some of the highest heels he'd even seen. And in fact, now that he was closer, he could see that her top was actually transparent!

His face hardened. Basically, she was sexy and she knew it.

So not his type at all—and yet he had followed her.

Still not entirely sure why he had done that, but somehow reluctant to leave, Luis shrugged off his jacket and pushed his way to the front of the bar.

'Una sin.'

At least that was something that had changed

for the better in the five years since he'd been away. Alcohol-free beer was widely available now, and an acceptable substitute for the real thing.

Not that it would have made any difference if it hadn't been. He would drink dishwater rather than break his vow. Never again would he risk that loss of control that had ripped his world apart.

Staring straight ahead, he lifted the glass to his lips. He had deliberately chosen to sit with his back to the red-haired woman, and she should have been out of sight and out of mind. But, despite not actually being able to see her, he could still sense her every move. Could picture her hand reaching up to tuck her hair behind her ear, almost hear that soft, sexy laugh that hinted not just at fun and flirtation but at a fantasy come true.

Annoyed with the direction of his thoughts, but unable to stop himself, he looked up at the mirror above the bar, his eyes fixing on her reflection. Instantly he regretted his lack of self-control, for she was laughing at something one of the men was saying, her hand brushing against his arm as she leaned in closer to him.

Luis scowled. No doubt he was her boyfriend—for now. The rest were just watching and waiting. Or maybe *she* was watching and waiting to see which of the men in the room were prepared to make a move.

His eyes narrowed and he felt a swirling anger mingle with his desire as he realised that he himself was included in that demographic.

Why, then, did he find her so damn desirable?

It didn't make any sense that someone like him would be attracted to someone like her—especially not now. Tonight of all nights he needed to stay detached. Yet, like a bull mesmerised by that flash of red, he could feel himself being drawn to her.

He ran his hand wearily over his face. It must be tiredness…or the heat.

Right, he mocked himself. Or maybe, like every other man within a five-mile radius, he wanted what she was offering.

Glancing over his shoulder at the group of men, he felt his chest tighten. Even from here he could feel their longing, spilling into the dark club.

Like it or not, he was no different.

His heartbeat slowed. Except that he was.

Sure, he'd had girlfriends. No one special, though. And nor was there likely to be any time soon, for more than anything he needed to be certain—and certainty was not a part of the dating equation. Chasing women was definitely not his thing either. It was Bas who had loved the thrill of the chase.

His hand tightened involuntarily around the glass.

The thrill of the chase—even just thinking the words made him feel slightly sick and, tilting his glass, he gazed down at the swirling contents and tried to distract himself from the guilt and remorse building inside his chest.

It didn't work. And suddenly he knew that it was time to leave. That his little adventure was over.

Keeping his eyes low, he breathed out softly, then still clutching his glass, he turned and—

The glass slammed against his chest, beer slopping down his T-shirt.

He heard a soft cry of surprise, and then the reflexes honed by years of riding motorbikes kicked in. Reaching out, he grabbed the arm flailing in front of him just as his startled brain realised that it was *her*—the red-haired woman.

Cristina Shephard gasped.

One moment she'd been taking a selfie on her phone—the next she was falling forward. Her one conscious thought was, *I knew I shouldn't have worn these heels*, and then suddenly, out of nowhere, she was being pulled upright, strong hands curving around her wrist and waist.

She breathed out in a rush as those same hands spun her round. 'Sorry…'

Why was she apologising? she thought dazedly, almost forgetting to breathe. He'd walked into *her*. But she knew why, and as her fingers curled into warm, hard muscle she gazed up at the man in front of her.

All evening she'd been aware of him. How could she not be? He dominated the whole club—and not just because he was handsome in a way that made you look twice...actually, three times. First to check you weren't seeing things. Then to marvel at such blatant perfection. And finally just to savour his extraordinary masculine beauty.

He was just so cool. With or without the leather jacket, he had an aura of calm assurance that suggested he was bigger than the sum of his problems. Or hers.

Although obviously not *hers*. She might never have shared them with anyone, but she knew her problems were too much for most people to handle. Or maybe it was her that was the problem. Her last boyfriend had more or less told her that—shortly after she'd found him in bed with her flatmate.

Her stomach clenched and, pushing aside that thought, she said quickly, 'Thank you for catching me—and sorry about your beer.'

Luis stared at her. Up close, she was more than beautiful. She was devastatingly lovely. Her huge, melting *turrón*-coloured eyes with their fringe of probably fake eyelashes were perfectly offset by her flushed cheeks and the scarlet bow of her mouth. He wondered just how soft the skin was on her throat, and then instantly wished that he hadn't as his brain began tugging him on an imaginary tour beneath her clothing.

Imposing an indifference he didn't feel onto his features, he shrugged. 'I was leaving anyway.'

Looking down into her beautiful, curious face, he couldn't actually remember why that was the case. In fact he appeared to be having trouble re-membering how to do a lot of things—like breath-ing and speaking. It was her fault, though, he thought irritably. Her beauty kept catching him off guard, so that each time he looked at her he forgot what he'd been planning to say.

As the silence grew, Cristina felt her lungs con-tract.

What was she doing here?

Tomorrow was going to be the biggest day of her life and she should be back in her hotel room, having a quiet night in on her own—just as she'd promised her mum. Only 'quiet and alone' were not a great combination, for that was when the thoughts came creeping into her head—thoughts that left her breathless with misery and doubt.

And so she'd come out, bumped into some peo-ple at a bar, and ended up here.

With him.

Her mouth felt dry and her breath was sud-

denly scratchy in her throat. It actually hurt to
look at him.

She'd been surrounded by men all evening, but
none of them had felt real. They were like cha-
meleons—constantly changing according to their
environment. It had made her feel nervous and
unsteady, as though the solid floor of the club was
actually quicksand.

Her heart tripped in her chest.

And then there was this man.

She liked it that he had ignored the dress code.
Liked it, too, that he was happy with his own
company. Not that he needed to be. She wasn't
the only women in the club who'd clocked him—
for obvious reasons.

He definitely ticked all the boxes in the 'tall,
dark and handsome' category. In fact his hair was
almost black, and so long it curled loosely over
the collar of his now damp T-shirt. Stubble that
was definitely not 'designer' shadowed the clean
lines of his jaw, and he had a small infinity tat-
too on his wrist.

How on earth had he got past the *gorilas* on the
door? she wondered distractedly. Even *she'd* had
trouble getting in.

But probably he'd just walked straight in. Men
with his kind of aura didn't stop for doormen.

Aware suddenly that she had been staring
at him for what felt like for ever, she glanced

down at his almost empty glass and said quickly, 'Please. Have mine.'

She held out the bottle but he shook his head.

'Okay, then let me buy you another one? To make up for spilling yours.'

Pulse racing, she reached into her bag, pulled out her purse and—

'Oh.'

Groaning inwardly, she gazed down at the handful of coins. She'd meant to go to the cashpoint on her way out but she'd forgotten.

'It really doesn't matter.'

He spoke quietly, but there was a firmness to his voice that cut through his casual manner and made her breathing accelerate in time with her heartbeat.

'It does.' She cleared her throat. 'Look, Tomás will buy you one. He won't mind.'

Luis gazed at her incredulously. He could hardly believe what she'd just said.

Seriously? She was going to ask her boyfriend to buy him a drink?

His face hardened. 'There's no need, really,' he said tersely.

He didn't care about the drink. Or his T-shirt. Or the fact that she had a boyfriend. He definitely didn't care about that, he thought angrily. So why, then, did he feel so wound up?

And then, catching sight of the phone in her

hand, he felt a warm surge of relief. She'd been taking a selfie—that was why she'd bumped into him.

Wasn't it enough that every man in the room was drooling all over her? Did she have to drool over herself too?

Reaching around her, he snatched up his leather jacket from the bar stool.

'I don't want another drink,' he said quietly. 'But just do yourself and everyone else a favour and look where you're going next time you come over all narcissistic.'

She gazed up at him as if she couldn't quite believe what he was saying. Probably she couldn't. With lips and legs like hers she'd almost certainly never had to take responsibility for her actions before.

Her mouth curled. 'I *was* looking where I was going because I was standing still. *You* walked into me.'

It was true. He had walked into her. But somehow the knowledge that he was technically in the wrong just antagonised him more.

His voice cold, and clipped with a fury he didn't fully understand, he shrugged his arms into his jacket. 'You were taking a selfie in the middle of a nightclub. You weren't concentrating. And that's how accidents happen.'

He watched her eyes darken to the colour of

burnt sugar, her face stiffening with shock and then a fury that doused his.

'Well, don't worry—next time I spill a drink all over you I'll make sure I do it on purpose.'

She stared at him fiercely and then, lifting her chin, turned and stalked off towards the dance floor.

For a fraction of a second Luis stared after her, his heart ricocheting inside his chest. Then, biting down on the frustration rising inside his throat, he turned and strode towards the stairs.

Out in the street, he felt his fury fade in the still night air. Gazing up at the dark sky, he breathed out slowly.

He hated conflict of any kind. Rarely lost his temper or provoked a fight. Yet tonight he'd almost done both—and with a woman. Gritting his teeth, he cursed softly. He'd been obnoxious and childish—and frankly he'd deserved everything she'd thrown at him and more.

In fact he was lucky she hadn't thrown her own drink at him too, he thought savagely as he began walking across the square.

The pavements were empty now, almost like a ghost town, and he felt a wrench of loneliness as he unlocked his bike. He missed Bas so much. Living in California, it was easy to rationalise his brother's absence from his life. All he had to do was pretend that back in Spain Bas was doing just what he always did—teasing their mother, eating *empanadas* by the plateful, partying until dawn with his friends.

Here, though, it was impossible to pretend.

And it would be even harder tomorrow—he glanced at his watch and frowned—or rather later today, with his parents. His stomach twisted with guilt and grief, and suddenly he knew that he had to move.

Straddling the bike, he pushed the key clumsily into the ignition. It would better once he was moving. On the open road, with the sound of the engine mingling with the beat of his blood, his feelings would spin away into the darkness like the dirt beneath his wheels.

He eased the bike forward and turned the ignition. Pulling in the clutch, he thumbed the starter button—and then frowned as the engine sputtered and died.

Damn it!

He tried again, and then again, over and over, feeling a tic of irritation start to pulse in his cheek. What the hell was wrong with the damn thing? It made no sense.

Trying to stay calm, he leaned forward and took a deep breath. He would check the blindingly obvious. And then…

And then nothing. For anything else he'd need pliers, a wrench, a screwdriver—

'Do you need any help?'

He sensed movement behind him and, turning, he felt his breath catch in his throat as she took a step closer.

She was watching him warily. Her auburn hair was now tied up into some kind of messy ponytail and she'd changed her shoes. Glancing at the black military-style boots on her feet, he almost smiled. Good job she hadn't been wearing those earlier or he might not have made it out the club.

He shook his head. 'Not sure you can,' he said carefully. Holding her gaze, he gestured towards the high-heeled shoes dangling from her hand. 'Unless those transform into some kind of toolkit. Or are you planning on throwing *them* at me too?'

Cristina stared at him in silence.

She had hesitated before coming over. He'd been so patronising and rude to her. But then she had spilled his drink over him, so maybe that made them equal. It was a pretty lame argument, but before her brain had had a chance to object she had already been walking across the square.

'I didn't plan on throwing your drink over you—as you yourself pointed out. Now, do you want my help or not?'

Luis stared at her for a long moment. Her voice

was husky—distractingly so. Was this some kind of trick? Or a joke.

'You want to help me?' he said slowly. 'I'm—'

'Touched?' she suggested. 'Grateful? Pleased?'

'Actually, I was going to say surprised. And a little nervous maybe.' He glanced over at her shoes.

Her mouth twitched. 'Well, I probably would have broken my leg or my neck if you hadn't caught me, so I guess it's only fair.'

'It's more than fair. It's magnanimous, given that I not only walked into you but then failed to apologise for doing so.' His grey eyes were level with hers. 'I'm sorry. I was the one who wasn't looking where I was going.'

As his gaze held hers Cristina felt her heart thud against her ribs. Even though it had been a little awkward, she liked that he had picked up where they had left off. Liked that he was honest enough to admit that he'd been wrong.

And, although he might not say much, she liked that he meant what he said.

'Don't you need to get home?'

Home. The word made her breathe in sharply. She shrugged.

'Right now, I don't really have one. I'm just travelling.'

Feeling suddenly horribly self-conscious, she glanced down at the Ducati.

'I don't know this model, but I'm almost sure you don't need a toolkit to fix it.'

Watching his mouth turn up at one corner, she felt a rush of heat tighten her skin. It was impossible not to imagine what he would look like if he smiled properly, or what it would be like to be kissed by that mouth.

Feeling his gaze on her face, and terrified that her thoughts might somehow be visible, she frowned. 'Did I say something funny?'

'No, I'm just tweaking my mental picture of you. I had you down as a party girl, not a back-warmer.'

She took a step towards him, her eyes narrowing. 'Is that right? Then maybe what you need isn't a toolkit but a little imagination. Or perhaps a little less prejudice. Women ride motorbikes on their own these days, and guess what? They don't even do it side saddle.'

Meeting her gaze, Luis felt something soft and dark stir inside in his blood as she took another step closer and touched the fuel tank between his legs.

He sighed. 'You're enjoying this.'

She nodded. 'A little. You were pretty mean to me.'

Watching her fingers stroke the warm gleaming metal, he felt his stomach tense.

'Is this some kind of hands-on healing?'

Her fingers stilled and she cleared her throat. 'Your bike is really clean. In comparison to your boots, I mean.'

They both looked down at his scuffed and dust-covered boots.

Despite himself, he was interested now. 'Okay, Nancy Drew, I got my bike washed this evening. And, no, it's not something I do very often but I have done it historically and I've never had a problem. And besides, it worked fine when I rode over here tonight.'

'Was it washed by hand?'

He frowned. 'No—pressure-wash.'

She nodded. 'Okay…well, I could be wrong, but water might have got into the ignition switch. It probably just needs a spritz of some kind of water-displacer.'

He stared at her, his pulse jumping with excitement, his hands tightening in a gesture of pure possession. He wanted her as he had never wanted any woman. Only the fact that, however deserted it appeared to be, they were still in a public place stopped him from reaching out and—

Stomach clenching with desire, he pushed aside an image of her splayed against the gas tank and said dryly, 'That's good to know. But as I don't have any—'

He broke off in disbelief as she opened up her handbag and pulled out a small spray can.

'I know how this must look, but I don't normally carry this stuff around with me,' she said quickly. 'It's just that the window in my hotel room is so squeaky that I can't sleep. Anyway, I complained, and when I was going out this evening the guy in reception gave me this.' She held out the can. 'It's worth a try.'

Luis wanted to ask her to rewind and repeat everything she'd just said, but instead he took the can and sprayed the ignition switch. He waited a moment, and then turned the key. He grinned as the snarl of the engine punctured the silence in the square.

Cristina blinked, and then smiled too. It was impossible not to. For, even though it was a dark and starless night, his smile made her feel as though the sun was rising and it was a new dawn.

She felt her heart skip a beat.

No wonder she'd tripped earlier.

Since finding Dominic, her on-off boyfriend of several months, in bed with her flatmate, she'd sworn off men. But there were men and then there was fate.

And surely that was why she had spilt his drink over him. Why his bike had failed to start. And why she'd ended up booking the worst hotel in Segovia, possibly in Spain.

'Thank you.'

He was holding out the can to her.

'It's okay. You can keep it.'

'But your window—'

'It's fine. I probably won't sleep tonight anyway. My mattress is really hard, and I think it's going to storm later. It's so hot and humid now.'

Luis felt his body tense. *Hard. Hot. Humid.* Why did every word she said make him think of sex?

Gritting his teeth, he ignored the blood pounding through his veins and forced himself to speak. 'So how did you know what was wrong?'

Cristina hesitated. *Good question.* However, the completely truthful answer was not one she was about to share with a perfect stranger—no matter how tall, dark and handsome.

It would take too long, and—her skin tightened over her cheekbones—it would be too humiliating to reveal the mend-and-make-do life she and her mother had been forced to live for so many years. But, just as she always did, she would tell him one truth.

Her eyes met his. 'My dad had a motorbike. Not like this one, but I took it over for a bit and I got to hang out with bikers—and they can't shut up about ignitions and sparks.'

She winced inside. What was she doing, rambling on about bikers as if she was some kind of Hell's Angel?

'Anyway…' She glanced up at the sky. 'I should

probably be going. It's late, and I want to get back to my hotel before it starts to rain.'

That wasn't true. The thought of her bedroom, dark and quiet, filled her with dread. She didn't want to be alone. But tonight was not the night to mess up, and how could taking this handsome stranger back to her room be anything but a risk not worth taking?

She held out her hand. 'Goodbye,' she said woodenly.

He took it, and at the touch of his fingers heat flared inside of her—and something bittersweet. A sense of what might have been if they'd met at some other time.

'Let me give you a lift. Please. It's the least I can do.'

His voice jolted her back to reality and, swallowing down the ache in her throat, she shook her head.

'No, really—it's fine.' She pointed at one of the side streets off the square. 'My hotel is literally down there.'

He looked at her for the longest time, then frowned.

'I don't even know your name.' He sounded surprised.

'It's Cristina.'

He nodded. 'Lucho.'

There was a low rumble of thunder overhead,

and as they both looked up at the sky she took a deep breath. 'You should go or you'll get soaked.'

He nodded and dropped her hand, and quickly, before she could change her mind, she turned and began to walk away as the rain started to fall.

At first it was soft and light like tears but then almost immediately it changed. Heavy, fat droplets hammered her head and shoulders so that in seconds she was soaked and the pavement was awash with water.

Don't look back, she told herself. *This wasn't meant to be. Just keep walking.*

But she couldn't just walk away. And, really, what difference would it make if she took one last look?

She turned, and suddenly her heart was hammering louder than the rain.

He was still sitting there, watching her, rain running down his face.

Cristina shivered.

He was waiting.

For her.

For a moment she hesitated.

Don't—don't go back. It's just because you're nervous about tomorrow, and when you get nervous you make stupid decisions.

Her heart kicked against her ribs, and then she walking, running back across the square, and what she was feeling wasn't nervousness but relief. And then he was pulling her against him, his mouth seeking hers, his hands sliding beneath the soaking fabric of her top.

They left the bike where it was, and ran to her hotel. Ignoring the startled glance of the receptionist, they stumbled up the stairs and into her bedroom.

He kicked the door shut and, bending his head, he took her mouth again. Rising on tiptoe, she kissed him back, her fingers tugging at his T-shirt, her mouth meeting his with urgent, frantic hunger.

'No—' Her eyes darkened with frustration as he broke away from her mouth and yanked his T-shirt over his head.

He was so gorgeous—all sleek, hard muscle and smooth skin, and a line of soft dark hair disappearing into the waistband of his jeans.

Reaching out, she ran her fingers lightly over the hair, watching his muscles tremble, and then she breathed in sharply as he took hold of the zip on the front of her jacket and slowly pulled it down.

Leaning forward, he rested his forehead against hers, the dark grey of his eyes almost black. For an endless moment he stared at her, his breathing ragged, and then, lowering his mouth, he began to kiss her again—lips, neck, throat—each kiss leading on to the next one and the next.

As he buried his face against her neck she moaned softly, sliding her fingers up through his hair. Her head was spinning…heat was slipping over her skin as his hands slid under her top, under the bandeau she was wearing underneath and over her damp breasts, his thumbs caressing the hard peaks of her nipples.

For the second time that night her legs crumpled beneath her, and her fingers tightened in his hair.

She heard a hiss as he breathed in sharply, and then he was tugging down her shorts, lifting her up, his hands curving beneath her as he pinned her against the door with his body. She shifted against him, panting, seeking relief for the ache building inside her, until suddenly she couldn't bear it any longer and her fingers clawed at his belt and zip, pushing his jeans down.

'Wait…' he muttered, and she felt her breath catch as he fumbled in his pocket and slid a condom on.

For a moment he held her gaze, and then, groaning, he forced her mouth back to his. Pushing aside the fabric of her panties, he thrust inside her. She arched against him, her nails biting into his arms, and then her muscles clenched and she cried out with pleasure as his body shuddered and slammed into her.

CHAPTER TWO

EVEN BEFORE SHE opened her eyes Cristina knew that Lucho was gone.

Shifting down beneath the duvet, she gazed up at the ceiling. From the sharpness of the light creeping beneath the curtains, and the buzz of traffic in the street, she guessed that it was probably time to get up.

And she *would* get up—only not just yet. For getting up would mean having to accept that what had happened last night was over, and she wasn't quite ready to do that.

Closing her eyes, she rolled on to her side.

Her body felt pleasurably blurred at the edges, and her lips were still tingling. Lifting a hand to her mouth, she touched it lightly, feeling her lips curve into a smile as she remembered everything.

A wild, breathless happiness was swirling inside her. She could hardly believe that any of it was real. Meeting him in the club, spilling his drink, following him outside and his bike refusing to start—

Groaning, her cheeks suddenly burning, she

buried her face in the pillow, remembering how she'd pulled that can from her handbag…

Her pulse stumbled.

And then the storm had started. Thunder—and rain like a monsoon.

He'd been soaked to the skin.

But he had waited for her.

The heat on her cheeks spread as another memory came to her. Of her body anchored to his… and of his dark, steady gaze watching her until the moment he'd buried his beautiful face in her neck and shuddered deep inside her.

She shivered, remembering, her thighs pressing together, pressing against the warmth and the tenderness there.

That had been the first time…

Later, after she'd lost count of the number of times and ways they'd made love, he'd pulled her against him, his eyes still dark, but soft with sleep, and kissed her gently.

She bit her lip. His intensity, his stamina, his skill hadn't surprised her. But that kiss had. Or maybe her response to it was what was so surprising.

She'd never felt like that with any man before. She had wanted him so badly. Her need for him had been fierce and absolute and unstoppable—like a river breaking its banks. And he had needed her too. She had never felt so wanted, so desired.

Opening her eyes, she bit her lip. Or so certain.

Normally, even the thought of intimacy with a man triggered a loop of self-doubt and distrust inside her head, so that she was already questioning her behaviour and possible responses before anything had even happened.

Her mouth twisted. And for good reason.

She'd only had a handful of relationships, but they'd all ended the same way—with whatever boyfriend it had been telling her that she was too difficult, too demanding. In other words nothing like the carefree young woman they had fallen for.

After what had happened with Dominic she'd given up. It was easier that way. Easier and less exhausting than caring about someone only to be inevitably let down.

And she'd stuck to her pledge.

Until last night.

But she didn't regret it. Lucho had been a great lover. He had made her feel desirable and sexy. Okay, he hadn't said much, but she was glad about that for last night she hadn't wanted to talk.

And if they had talked she would have been busy now picking over his words.

Rolling over, she pulled one of the pillows towards her and hugged it against her stomach, the faint lingering scent of his cologne making her think of night and heat and rain about to fall.

Lucho hadn't needed to talk. To big himself up. Why would he?

He was gorgeous. All lustrous golden skin and lean muscle, and those dark eyes that had seemed to swallow her whole.

And she liked the fact that he had been happy to communicate through touch, his fingers writing poems on her body, his warm breath against her throat a wordless promise of infinite pleasure. His silence had nothing to do with laziness or shyness, but contentment. He was one of those rare people who was happy living in the moment, without expectations or regrets and with nothing to prove.

Unlike her.

Picturing the remote expression on her father's face, the distance in his eyes, she curled her fingers into the pillow. He had not only managed to deny her existence, he'd replaced her too.

Her stomach flip-flopped as beneath her pillow the alarm buzzed on her phone. Reaching round, she switched it off, glancing at the screen. There were several missed calls, all from a number she didn't recognise, and for one brief moment she considered calling back.

But now was not a good time. For a start, she needed to shower, pack and get dressed, and she also wanted to check in with her boss. She trusted Grace—not just professionally, but on a personal level too—and she wanted to see if she had any last-minute advice for her.

And anybody who mattered would call her back if it was important. Not that whatever he or she was calling about was likely to be life-changing.

Rolling out of bed, she grabbed a towel and walked into the bathroom.

In another bathroom, on the other side of the city, Luis stepped out of the shower and wrapped a towel around the taut muscles of his stomach. Ignoring the mirror on the wall, he ran his hands slowly through his hair, smoothing the tangles with his fingers.

He released a slow breath, remembering how just hours earlier Cristina had done more or less the same thing. Except her hands had been urgent, frantic. Almost as frantic as her mouth.

His lungs emptied slowly. And she'd tasted so sweet…sweeter than molasses.

It was supposed to have been just sex—a carnal union designed to delight and, more importantly, to distract him from his thoughts. Except that now he couldn't stop thinking about her. And even though he knew she was in a hotel on the other side of the city, her presence was so strong in his memory that he kept turning to look at the bed, expecting to see her there.

Watching Cristina in the club had been one of the most confusing experiences of his life. She had dazzled him. Even just looking at her in those heels and that top, those shorts, had made a pulse of excitement beat beneath his skin. He had wanted her—and yet he'd almost hated her too. For she was *too* beautiful, *too* sexy, and an attention-seeker to boot. In other words, everything he loathed in a woman.

And so he'd got up to leave—

Gazing at his reflection, he felt his face grow warm.

She might have spilt his drink but she'd been right. It had been his fault. He'd been so desperate to leave that he hadn't been thinking about anything but getting as far away as possible from her gravitational pull. He certainly hadn't been looking where he was going.

Breathing in sharply, he ran his hand slowly over the stubble grazing his face.

Only instead of apologising he'd acted like a jerk.

His heartbeat slowed. He had lost her then, and that might have been the end of it—would have been if his bike hadn't refused to start.

He stared at his reflection, steadying himself, pushing aside the thought of what might have happened, or rather *not* happened, if his bike hadn't been washed or she hadn't come outside.

But she had, and she'd rescued him.

He swallowed.

Rescued him and then kissed him.

Or were they one and the same thing?

Glancing out of the window, he felt his heartbeat accelerate. He was naturally cautious by nature, but even if he hadn't been life had taught him in the most brutal and devastating way not to act impulsively. He didn't do spur-of-the-moment or random.

Yet last night he'd done both. Only instead of regret or shame he could feel a kind a radiance inside his chest. It took him a moment to realise that it was happiness, and that for the first time since stepping off the plane in Athens he was ready to face his past.

Picking up his phone, he punched in a number. 'Carlos. It's Luis…'

Having settled his bill, he made the hotel's owner day by giving him his bike, and then, having finally extricated himself from the man's grateful and disbelieving embrace, he strolled down the street towards the *peluquería*.

It was just opening, and the old guy who ran it seemed slightly astonished to have a customer so early, but he was happy to do what Luis asked.

Thirty minutes later Luis stepped out into the sunshine, his dark hair cropped close to the head, his face smooth. Catching sight of himself in the window, he felt a flicker of panic. He looked so young. Almost as though the last five years had never happened.

Only so much *had* happened. So much he could never change. He ran his hand slowly over his jawline. The last time he'd been clean shaven had been for his brother's funeral.

It hadn't been a conscious decision to stop shaving—he'd just found it so hard to look at himself as life—*his life*—had carried on.

He had set up a hedge fund, a lucrative, global business. And he'd bought a house—several, actually. He'd even had the occasional girlfriend.

But none of it had mattered. None of it had felt real. Without Bas there to tease him about his tie, or drag him out at the end of a busy week, he'd felt empty, hollow.

Until last night.

With Cristina.

Picturing her beneath him, her eyes darkening as he'd thumbed her legs apart, he almost lost his footing on the pavement. Her passion had been primal; it had blindsided him, left him grappling for breath and self-control.

Over his shoulder, he felt rather than saw a dark saloon car peel away from the opposite side of the square and head towards him. For a moment he carried on walking, and then, slowing down, he turned and waited as the car drew up beside him.

Before it had even come to a stop a thickset man wearing a dark grey suit stepped out onto the pavement and pulled open the back passenger door. Luis nodded at him and climbed inside.

'Thanks for picking me up, Carlos,' he said softly, turning his head towards the window. 'Now, let's go home.'

The journey took less time than he remembered, but it was still long enough for his stomach to turn over and inside out. As the car passed slowly beneath a large stone arch and into a courtyard he had a familiar glimpse of yellowed walls and tall windows, and then he was stepping onto the cobbled paving.

Trying to rein in the beating of his heart, Luis made his way through his childhood home. It might be five years since he'd been back, but he knew exactly where his parents would be waiting.

But he was wrong.

As he walked into the sitting room he frowned. It was empty.

It looked the same, though. He stared round dazedly, barely taking in the opulent interior with its beautiful tapestries and paintings by Goya and Velázquez. Only where were his mother and father?

Behind him a door opened softly and, turning, Luis felt his heart squeeze with a mixture of love, respect and dismay as a silver-haired man walked into the room.

His father, Agusto Osorio, might be nearly seventy, but he was still handsome. And his dark, austere grey eyes and upright bearing were a reminder that he was a man who was used to demanding and getting his way.

But although he was still tall, and immaculately dressed, there was a hesitancy and unsteadiness in his manner that hadn't been there before. Unable to watch his father's faltering progress any more, Luis crossed the faded Persian carpet and embraced the older man gently.

'Papá!'

His heart gave a lurch as he hugged the older man. His father smelt of shaving soap, and that old-fashioned cologne his mother loved, and there was a reassuring familiarity to his father's shoulders. As a child he'd loved to be carried up there; for a long time it had been the only way he could be taller than Bas.

His chest tightened as Agusto released him and smiled.

'We were expecting you earlier. Your mother was worried until she got your text. She misses you. We both do,' he said simply. 'It's good to have you home, Luis, even if it is just for a week.'

Trying to suppress the ache inside his chest,

Luis nodded. 'It's good to be back, Papá. And I'm sorry I can't stay longer—'

His father patted him on the arm. 'We understand.' He gestured towards a trio of sofas and armchairs. 'Sit! I'll ring for coffee.'

Watching his father's face crease in pain as he turned and tentatively lowered himself into one of the chairs, Luis held his breath. As a child, Agusto had seemed to him like one of the mythical knights in the books he'd used to read to his sons. A man of honour, vital, inviolate and invincible.

Now, though, his father looked frail and tried— smaller, somehow. Only it wasn't just the passing of time that had caused these changes, but the pain and grief of losing his oldest son.

He felt another stab of guilt and, glancing past him, said quickly, 'Where's Mamá? Should I go and find her?'

'You don't have to, *mi cariño*, I'm right here.'

Across the room, his mother Sofia was standing in the doorway. Before he'd even realised what he was doing he was on his feet and moving. As they embraced he felt a tug at his heart, for he could sense that she had changed more than his father. Not physically—she was still beautiful, slim and elegant—but her sadness was palpable. It seemed to seep into him so that he was suddenly struggling to breathe.

'Luis, you look so well. Doesn't he, Agusto?' She turned to her husband.

Smiling, Agusto nodded as the housekeeper arrived with a tray. 'Yes, he does, *querida*! Ah, here's the coffee. *Gracias*, Soledad. Just there will be perfect.'

Luis waited until they were alone again, and then, turning towards his mother, he smiled. 'So, how many people are coming to the party?'

'Sixty, of course—that's why we had to arrange it for tomorrow. It was the only date everyone could make. '

Picking up his coffee cup, Agusto cleared his throat. 'But we can always squeeze in one more if there's someone special you'd like to bring along.' He glanced over at his son. 'We did wonder if you might bring Amy.'

Shaking his head, Luis met his father's gaze with resignation. 'That's not going to happen, Papá. I haven't dated her in about a year. We're friends now—that's all.'

His father frowned at him. 'But you're seeing someone else?'

'No one serious.'

He held his breath, waiting for the conversation to continue as he knew it surely would. His parents had met at his mother's *quincañera*. It had been love at first sight, and they had both believed—assumed, really—that their sons would find a partner just as effortlessly.

Only with Bas gone all their attention was now focused on him, so that every conversation, no matter how it started, always seemed to turn inevitably to Luis's relationships. But he didn't—couldn't—trust his feelings. Believing that someone loved and desired you was stupid and dangerous. It lulled you into a dream state, made you careless.

And he was never careless. Never took risks. In fact he'd spent most of his adult life doing his damnedest to minimise risk, doing everything in his power to control the world around him. It was one of the reasons why he'd set up his business. Hedge funds were by definition speculative. However, by using algorithms to calculate the optimal probability of executing a profitable trade, he'd eliminated not just fear and greed but risk. Risks that were not worth taking—

His body stilled, his breath catching in his throat as he pictured Cristina, with those ludicrous heels dangling from her hand, as he'd kissed her up the stairs to her hotel room.

She'd been a risk worth taking.

He felt suddenly exhilarated, and a flurry of anticipation rose up inside him.

A risk worth repeating.

He would call her hotel after lunch.

Feeling calmer, he glanced over at his father. 'Life is different in California, Papá. The people are different there. They don't care about—'

'About what? Love? Commitment? Family?'

He could hear the confusion in his father's voice, and the hurt. About everything that was left unspoken. The past. His brother. And, of course, the family business.

His father was coming up to seventy. He wanted to retire and he wanted Luis to take over from him. But he wasn't going to. He couldn't step in for his brother. Sit at the head of that massive oak table in the boardroom. It just wasn't going to happen.

Glancing at his father expression of frustration and his mother's stricken face, he wanted to apologise for letting them down. For not being the son they deserved. But to do so would mean having to explain his reasons, and that would mean losing their love for ever.

His father shook his head. 'Thank goodness we're only being photographed for this article,' he muttered. 'I can't imagine how I'd explain the fact that my only son and heir has turned his back on his birthright.'

Luis felt his skin tighten across his face, his brain locking on to the one word in his father's remark that was designed to trigger alarm bells in his head.

'What article?'

Sofia leaned forward. 'It's for a magazine. We're meeting the photographer before lunch, just to have a little chat. I have her CV here…'

Reaching across, she picked up a folder from the table, and handed it to Luis.

He didn't open it.

'But what's the point of the article?' He could feel his hackles rising.

His father raised an eyebrow. 'I know you're not interested in the family business, Luis. But I would have thought that even *you* might have remembered it's the bank's four hundredth anniversary this year.'

Luis cursed silently. Of course it was. Agusto had mentioned it to him several months back. Believing it to be some kind of entrée into discussing his return to the family business, he'd pushed it away.

Gritting his teeth, he forced himself to speak calmly. 'I hadn't forgotten, Papá,' he said slowly. 'I just didn't connect the dots.' He frowned. 'I get that the anniversary is a big deal, but Banco Osorio's reputation is built on our discretion. We never talk to the media. So why go public now?'

'It was my idea.' His mother looked up at him, her face suddenly anxious. 'Do you think I made a mistake, Luis?'

Damn right he did. He didn't trust any journalists or photographers.

But he could hardly explain the reason for that to his parents.

His spine stiffened, his body tensing as memories filled his head. Memories of the night his brother had died.

He hadn't even wanted to go to that party, only Bas had insisted and his mother had backed him up. She knew that Luis needed his big brother in order to socialise, and Bas needed Luis to rein in his excesses.

But the party had been so not his style. Wall-to-wall trust fund brats, drinking and whining about their parents.

Watching Bas work the party, Luis had felt one of his occasional twinges of envy. His brother was so charming. With Bas there he always felt like a spare part—particularly around women. Then, out of nowhere, he'd spotted her. And she had been looking at *him*.

Unlike all the other women in the room, she'd looked at ease with herself. Jeans, boots, hair loose to her shoulders. They had talked and talked, shouting at first, over the noise of the party, and then later more quietly out on the balcony. She had liked the same artists he did, hated parties, and had had an older sister who was much cooler than she was.

He had felt as though she knew him inside out. It was only later that he'd realised why that was. Much later.

After he'd slept with her.

After he'd learnt that she was a *paparazza* and after he'd accidentally let slip where Bas was going to be staying that night.

After her colleagues had chased his brother to his death.

Striving for calm, he looked up at his mother. 'So when is this photo shoot happening?'

'Next week. The day after you go back to California.' Sofia bit her lip. 'Your father wasn't sure, but he's worked so hard and I wanted to do something—'

He squeezed his mother's hand gently. 'It's a lovely idea.'

He felt a fist of tension curl inside his stomach.

He couldn't stay. It would be unbearable, and unfair to his parents, for he knew they would begin to talk wistfully of his moving back to Spain.

But how could he leave them to face some unscrupulous photographer alone? They were so otherworldly, so trusting.

'I know you don't like the press,' his mother said tentatively. 'But we'll have final say over the photos. And your father made it clear that we won't be answering personal questions.'

There was a knock on the door. It was Soledad.

'The photographer is here, Señor Osorio. She's waiting in the *salón azul*.'

'Thank you, Soledad.'

Taking his mother's hand, Luis helped her to her feet. 'I feel bad about making such a fuss, Mamá. Let me come with you—please. I might even be some help. I deal with the media a lot back in California, so I'm pretty sure I can handle anything they throw at me.'

His words were still reverberating around his head as he followed his father into the *salón azul* and came face to face with Cristina.

He stared at her in silence, his heartbeat deafeningly loud, a thousand questions bombarding his brain.

Had he just looked at her clothes he might not have recognised her. Gone were the denim shorts and that insane transparent top. Instead she was wearing tailored navy trousers and a blue-and-white-striped matelot top. Only her hair was the same—still tumbling over her shoulders in a mass of glossy red waves.

Slowly the events of the night before began to whirl in front of his eyes, spinning over and over until finally they lined up alongside one another like fruit on a slot machine.

Drink. Bike. Kiss.

Jackpot.

His breath felt sharp in his throat as he realised that it had all been a set-up. Right from the moment he'd walked into that club he'd been played. Everything that had felt so random, so spontaneous—their eyes meeting in the mirror, her banging into him and spilling his drink, even her having that stupid can of oil in her bag—all of it had been planned.

Flipping open the folder his mother had given him, he read swiftly through her CV, his stomach knotting with fury both with her and himself.

What was wrong with him? After what had happened with Bas did he really need another opportunity to prove how naive and complacent he was?

Apparently he did.

Apparently he had already forgotten that a beautiful woman always had an agenda of her own.

He was on the verge of striding across the room and dragging her lying, manipulative little body out of the building, when his mother stepped past him, smiling.

'You must be Cristina. Welcome to our home.'

Sliding to her feet, Cristina held out her hand.

Her editor, Grace, had warned her that the Osorios were old-school and preferred to keep things on a formal footing, so she'd tried to dress in a way that implied she was professional, yet creative. But her heart was still beating like a startled horse as the beautiful grey-haired woman crossed the room towards her.

'Señora Osorio. Thank you so much for meeting me today.'

'Please…' Sofia smiled. 'You must call me Sofia. This is my husband, Agusto, and my son, Luis. He's over on a visit from California. Flew in this morning.'

Cristina shook Agusto's hand, and then, finally registering the second, taller, darker-haired man, she turned to Luis.

She smiled. Or tried to. But her lips wouldn't work. Her whole body seemed to be numb. Around her the room was dissolving into a mist the same grey as his eyes—*Lucho's* eyes—as silently she racked what was left of her brain for some kind of practical response to what was happening.

Only Grace's notes had said nothing about coming face to face with your one-night stand. Or finding out he was the son of the people you were meant to photograph.

As he held out his hand she took it mechanically.

It couldn't be.

Except that it was, and suddenly she thought she might faint.

Sofia was staring at her. 'Are you all right, my dear? You look pale.'

'I'm fine.' She smiled stiffly. 'Too much coffee, I'm afraid. I should probably try decaffeinated, but it's so disgusting. I prefer a simple *espresso*—Arabica bean, black, no sugar.'

Agusto beamed at her. 'Ah, a coffee connoisseur. I'm trying to cut back too, but it's hard when the alternatives are such poor substitutes.'

Cristina nodded, and then, sensing Luis's cool, dismissive gaze, she felt a rush of anger. 'I agree. I *hate* things that aren't what they appear to be.'

A warning flag of anger flared in his grey eyes, but she didn't care.

Lucho—Luis—whatever he called himself—was a phony, happy to offer different versions of himself in order to get what he wanted.

In this case her.

He was just like her father—and she should have known that.

A familiar feeling of doubt and panic was slipping over her skin. She felt her eyes tugged towards the door and escape.

Her pulse jerked. Escape from *what*? She had come here to put the past behind her. It was why she'd fought so hard to win this assignment. To make the world, and more particularly her father, sit up and take notice. And that was what would happen when she sent him a copy of the magazine with her byline beneath the photographs. Lifting her chin, she smiled at Agusto.

'I'm sure you didn't invite me here to discuss coffee. How about I talk you through the production process for the shoot? And then if you have any questions I'll try and answer them.'

'*I* have some questions.'

Luis's voice cut through her smile.

'You do?' She forced herself to meet his gaze. 'That's great,' she said stiffly.

'You seem very young. I'm just wondering about your experience.'

His mother frowned at him. 'I gave you Cristina's CV, *cariño*.'

'And I read it. It seems very light. Does it cover all your talents?'

He watched her beautiful light brown eyes widen.

'No, not all of them.' She looked at him calmly. 'I worked in a cake shop when I was fifteen, so I can make a mean *crème pâtissière* if you're tempted.'

'I'm not.' He held her gaze. 'Not any more, anyway.'

After the interview was over, and Cristina had left the room, Sofia glanced at her husband and son and said quickly, 'Well, I thought that went well. I know she's young, but she seemed very genuine—and quite charming.'

Luis felt his stomach twist. Oh, she was charming, all right—but *genuine*?

Breathing in, he said as calmly as he could manage, 'She did seem charming. But wouldn't you prefer someone with a little more gravitas?'

He was speaking to his mother, but it was his father who answered the question.

'Not really. Unless you have a particular reason to doubt this young women?'

Luis hesitated. *Say it*, he ordered himself. *Tell the truth.*

But how? He could hardly tell his mother that he'd had sex with Cristina. For a start, she thought he'd flown in that morning. Nor could he reveal that his fears lay rooted in a mistake he'd made five years ago—a mistake that had cost his brother his life and his parents a son.

Looking at their faces, he made up his mind. He didn't trust Cristina, but he didn't need to admit that or explain why. He just needed to be around to keep tabs on her.

Slowly, he shook his head. 'No, I don't. All that matters to me is that you're happy. And besides, I can help. You know how much I love photography.'

His mother looked at him in confusion. 'But, *cariño*, you won't be here—'

Luis picked up his mother's hand and pressed it to his mouth. 'I can be, Mamá. And I *want* to be.'

His mother's tears of happiness made him feel guiltier than ever. But he would do whatever it took to protect his parents. Even lie to them.

'I think it would be a good idea if we did the photo shoot on the island,' he said firmly.

La Isla de los Halcones had belonged to the Osorio family for over one hundred years. It was isolated—only accessible by motorboat—and best of all communication with the mainland was limited to a landline.

It's completely private, and much more relaxed.' He smiled reassuringly at both of them. 'It'll be perfect, and I'll be there to supervise the whole thing.'

And if that meant keeping a close eye on Cristina then so be it.

CHAPTER THREE

'Is there anything else I can get you, Ms Shephard? More coffee?'

Closing her laptop, Cristina smiled up at the air stewardess and shook her head. 'No, thank you. I'm good.'

The stewardess smiled back at her. 'Okay, but just let me know if you need anything.'

Watching the woman move gracefully away down the cabin, she resisted the urge to pinch herself again, and instead gazed out of the window at the cloudless blue sky.

She'd never flown business class before, and frankly it would probably be a long time before she did so again. But the Osorios had insisted, and it was a treat to have the extra legroom and a lunch that was actually edible.

The Osorio name had helped in other ways too. She'd been fast-tracked through baggage and security, and a limousine would be waiting at Valencia airport to take her to the marina.

It was all very civilised. But then people like Agusto and Sofia didn't queue for taxis or hang around waiting for luggage. The rich and the powerful valued their time almost as much as their privacy, and unlike normal people they only did what they wanted to do.

As she knew from experience.

She felt her face stiffen, the muscles tightening involuntarily, and, reaching down, she picked up her cup—china, not cardboard—and took a sip of coffee.

What other reason could there be for her father never bothering to get in touch with her?

Still gazing listlessly out of the window, she thought about how at the beginning she'd tried to make sense of his actions. Husbands divorced wives, not children, so why didn't he want to see her?

At first she'd made excuses for him, and then she'd blamed her mother. Later, though, there had been only one explanation. Her father didn't love her and he probably never had.

Frowning, Cristina flipped open her laptop and gazed determinedly down at the screen. She wasn't going to let her father's rejection ruin this moment for her. This was her last chance to do her final preparation before the photo shoot, and she wasn't going to waste it brooding about the past.

She began scrolling through the background notes that Grace had emailed to her. It didn't take long. It was mostly historical facts about the Osorio banking dynasty. Personal, biographical details about the family were frustratingly sparse.

Her heart gave a lurch. Panic was beginning to uncoil inside her stomach. It wasn't the first portrait that she'd taken—Grace wasn't *that* trusting. But it was the most important to date, and she wanted it to work. Not just for the magazine but for herself. She so badly wanted to prove that she could do this.

Her fingers shook slightly above the keyboard.

No, that wasn't true. She wanted more than that. She wanted to matter, to be somebody, to be noticed. And not just by her peers.

Only how could she do that if she couldn't find *the key to their story*?

She felt her stomach clench.

It was her job as a photographer to seek the truth—that was why she'd so foolishly become a *paparazza*. But with portraits the truth was elusive. In the intimacy of a studio-style setting people grew guarded, and of course there was always an obstacle between her camera and the sitter. It wasn't just a matter of point and click; the shutter was like a tiny little door that she needed to open.

And that required a key.

She had hoped to find one, talking to Agusto and Sofia. But although they had been polite, and helpful, they had fairly conservative ideas about what they wanted from the photo shoot—and, looking down at the pictures that Grace had sent her, she could see why.

To her photography was magic. But the Osorios were clearly intensely private people who simply wanted a record of a particular moment.

She needed to see beyond the staged poses. She needed to do a little supplementary research of her own. But as she typed in the Osorio name she felt heat spread over her cheeks as the screen filled not only with photos of Agusto and Sofia, but Luis too.

She stared at them greedily.

There were a couple of him as dark-eyed teenager, watching the polo at Sotogrande with his parents and brother. Another as a student in America, rowing at Harvard. And then, leaping forward several years, there were several more of the adult Luis. Publicity shots of him in his role as CEO of the quantitative hedge fund he'd founded.

Clearly turning his back on one fortune had been no obstacle to amassing another. His business was less than three years old but it had already made him a billionaire.

The thought of Luis behind a desk, with some glossy PA hovering over his shoulder, made her feel as if she was pressing on a bruise. But now that she knew the truth about him his career choice made perfect sense.

He enjoyed taking risks, was able to keep his

emotions in check, and clearly didn't mull over the consequences of his actions. Crucial qualities not just for succeeding in the high-stress, high-reward culture of the stock market, but for managing multiple lives.

So what if he was rich? Money wasn't everything.

Except when you didn't have it.

She gritted her teeth, familiar nausea cramping her stomach as she remembered the years of struggle after her father had deserted them.

He had left them penniless, and that had not been all. With no money coming into the house, and a terrifying number of bills to pay, there had been no time to deal with their shock and grief and anger.

But he'd probably never even given them or their feelings a thought. Why would he? After all, he'd relocated to America and just carried on as if nothing had happened.

As if *she* had never happened.

She had felt so unimportant. So insignificant.

Until last week, when Luis had walked into his parents' palatial living room and the expression on his face had confused and frightened her so much that she had forgotten to breathe.

She'd thought the shard of misery inside her chest would split her in two.

Luis Osorio was a liar. And a fake.

But—and it was an important 'but'—he also lived in California. And, despite barely managing to hold all the pieces of herself together during that awkward interview in Segovia, her brain had registered the fact that he was returning to the States at the end of the week—today, in fact.

Her shoulders straightened. She'd been right about him the first time in that club. He was a mistake. But now he was in her past. Here, in the present, it was just her and her camera.

Half an hour later the plane landed in Valencia. Feeling like a minor celebrity, she was whisked through the airport to the promised limousine, and then twenty minutes later was stepping onto a sleek, white motorboat.

Inside, the decor was all smooth, pale wood, cream leather upholstery and discreetly tinted glass. As she sat down in one of the armchairs she suddenly remembered that Agusto had referred to the boat as a 'dinghy'. Suppressing a smile, she was just about to pull out her camera when her phone rang.

'Chrissie, darling? It's not a bad time, is it?'

As usual, the tentative note in her mother's voice made her heart beat faster with love—and remorse.

Over the years she had been such a brat. More than anything she wanted to make amends, to show her mother how much she loved her. And if she did well with this assignment then finally it might be possible to do that with more than words. She might actually be able to give her mum the security of a home instead of just a couple of rooms that went with her job.

Clearing her throat, she said brightly, 'No it's a great time, Mum. I'm just on the boat now. On my way to the island.'

'How long does the ferry take?'

Her spine stiffened, her mother's innocent question catching her off-guard.

She hadn't lied—didn't lie, full-stop, not even about stupid, insignificant things. As far as she was concerned it was better to say nothing than to lie, and over the years she'd got really good at deflecting or misunderstanding anything that got too close to the bone.

So, no she hadn't lied, but she'd been reluctant to hint at the Osorios' insane wealth. With her history of messing up, she'd been scared of jinxing herself. But, knowing how excited her mother would be, she couldn't resist pressing the phone against her face, and whispering, 'It's their island, actually, and I'm not on a ferry. I'm on their motorboat.'

'A motorboat *and* a private island.' Her mother laughed. 'Oh, darling, it sounds like something from a film.' She hesitated. 'And will you be staying with the family?'

'Yes, they have a house there.' Actually Agusto had called it a fortress, but had he been speaking literally? 'I can't send you any pictures, though, Mum.'

'Of course not. I wouldn't—'

Cristina's phone buzzed. She frowned. Someone was trying to ring her.

She glanced at the screen, her eyes narrowing. Unknown number. *Damn!* Agusto had given her his private number but she hadn't had a chance to put it into her phone yet. Fumbling with her bag, she tried to find the notepad where she'd written it down.

'Mum, I'm going to have to go. I've got another call—'

'Oh, of course. Well, I'll hang up, then. Bye, darling, bye...'

Tucking the phone under her chin, Cristina cleared her throat.

'Cristina Shephard.'

But there was only silence. She cursed silently. She must have just missed it.

'Ms Shephard?'

Turning, her mind still on the mystery caller, she saw that it was one of the crew.

'We're just about to dock now. If you could stay seated until I return?'

Nodding, she managed a quick, tight smile.

Should she call back? No, she wouldn't—not

now. It would only distract her, and she needed to concentrate. Besides, if it was important they'd ring back, wouldn't they?

Stepping onto a short wooden jetty, she felt a flicker of anticipation ripple over her skin. She could taste the salt in the air, and as a slight breeze lifted her hair she couldn't stop herself from smiling.

Another limousine was waiting for her—only it was not the sort that could be rented out by the hour. Judging by the coat of arms on the door, it was the family's own private car. Settling back against the soft leather seating, she felt almost giddy with excitement. It was like being Cinderella.

Or maybe not Cinderella, she thought a moment later. There would be no fairy godmother or glass slipper to help her achieve her happy-ever-after. It was up to her to make this work.

Which was fine. She had the talent and the determination, so what could possibly stand in her way?

Turning her head, she gazed eagerly out of the window. For such a small island, there was quite a mix of landscapes. Inland, green hills covered with grass blended into dust-brown olive groves, like paint on a palette, while along the coastline clumps of pine trees ended in vertiginous drops down to the water. As the road twisted upwards

she could see that the cobalt blue sea splashed
foam up onto both shining dark rocks and sand
the colour of clotted cream.

There was a tiny church on one of the smaller
hills, and some rustic-looking cottages—and then
suddenly, as the car slid round a corner, she saw it.

Her mouth dropped open.

It really was a fortress.

Gazing up at the castellated stone walls, she
felt her heartbeat accelerate.

It was huge. The Osorios' beautiful home in
Segovia seemed modest in comparison, but even
the fortress was dwarfed by the six-sided tower
that rose up from the centre of the building.

Feeling almost hollow with shock and envy,
she was vaguely aware of the limousine stopping,
and then she was stepping out of the air-condi-
tioned cool into heat and sunlight. A middle-aged
woman wearing a cream linen dress greeted her
with a smile.

'Ms Shephard? Welcome to Fortaleza de Moya.
My name is Pilar, and I'm in charge of housekeep-
ing. I'll be taking care of you during your stay.'

Reining in her nerves, Cristina smiled. 'Thank
you. It's lovely to meet you.'

She glanced across at her shabby luggage, but
before she had a chance to move Pilar stepped
towards her.

'Javier will take your bags to your room. I'm

sure you want to freshen up after your long journey, but Señor Osorio was hoping you'd have a coffee with him first.'

Cristina held her gaze. It was difficult not to be intimidated by the opulence and glamour of the Osorios' world and their cool, crystalline confidence. Particularly when she dressed so casually.

But remembering Luis's cool dissection of her CV, she felt a rush of defiance. Now, more than anything, she wanted to get started. To prove that she could hold her own with these people.

Lifting her chin, she smiled. 'What a lovely idea. I could do with a coffee.'

She followed the other woman through a series of gorgeous, glamorous rooms out onto a stone balcony overlooking the sea. Coffee and some petit-fours were arranged on a marble-topped table, and after Pilar had left she picked up a small crescent-shaped biscuit and nibbled it—more for something to do than because she was hungry.

There was a slight breeze and, leaning forward against the balustrade, she drew up her mass of hair, enjoying the sensation of cool air on the warm skin of her neck.

Hearing footsteps behind her, she let her hair fall. Reminding herself to call him by his first name, she turned, smiling warmly.

'It's a beautiful view, Agusto. You must be so happy to see it—' she began.

But her words dried to dust in her mouth. For it wasn't Agusto standing there. It was his son, Luis, and he was looking anything but happy.

Luis stared at her, his heart pounding. Walking onto the balcony, he'd flinched. But not because of the glare of sunlight. It was looking at Cristina that had momentarily blinded him. With her auburn hair spilling down over her bare arms, her mouth open in an O of shock, she was easily as beautiful as the view she'd been admiring.

He felt a shot of anger; he wasn't sure if it was with her or with himself. But he was grateful that she was on the other side of the flagstones, for it took every step towards her for him to compose himself.

Although, to be honest, she looked more stunned than he felt.

Her words confirmed that fact as she said shakily, 'What are you doing here? Your father—'

'Isn't here.'

Her beauty felt like a punch to the face, but he held her gaze, forcing himself to look at her— *really* look at her—until the pain subsided to a dull ache.

'They arrive tomorrow. Something came up at the bank, so I offered to come along and hold the fort.'

Cristina stared at him mutely. If that was a joke,

it wasn't funny. But then humour was pretty low on her list of responses right now. Mostly she was in shock at coming face to face with him. And then there was the shock of his beauty.

Her pulse gave a twitch. She was used to beauty—had photographed numerous celebrities. None of them, though, had ever made her heart beat like a metronome. But then none of them had had a clear gold profile that could cut through the dusk of a summer evening.

He took a step towards her, his eyes drifting towards the biscuit in her hand.

'Making yourself at home, I see,' he said softly. 'Don't get too comfortable. You won't be staying.'

It took a moment for his words to sink in. Back in Segovia she'd thought he was warning her off, but this was the first time he'd made it clear.

'I'm pretty sure that's not up to you,' she said stiffly.

'Then you've been misinformed—or you have made an assumption based on ignorance, not fact. When I want something to happen, it does.'

'And let me guess…' She glared at him. 'You don't ask twice.'

She felt a chill slide over her skin as he shook his head, his grey eyes dark with hostility.

'I don't ask.' His gaze drifted dismissively over her face. 'You've had a nice all-expenses-paid trip. And now it's over.'

Holding on to her temper by a rapidly fraying thread, she raised an eyebrow. 'I don't work for you, and you have no say in what I do or where I do it. I do what my editor—'

'Really? Your editor told you to sleep with me?'

His face was cold and harsh.

Cristina gaped at him. Leaning over the balcony, lost in the sound of the waves and the heat of the mid-afternoon sun, she had been expecting a pleasant if slightly formal welcome from Agusto.

But Luis was neither pleasant nor welcoming. Nor did he bear any resemblance to the hard-muscled lover who had pulled her against him time and again during that night in the hotel. Instead he was staring at her in a way that made the solid stone beneath her feet feel flimsy.

'You surprise me. I've met your boss, and Grace Whiteley doesn't strike me as the kind of woman who'd pimp out her staff.'

'That's not I meant and you know it.' She was almost blindsided with outrage and fury. 'How dare you suggest that—?'

'That what? That you seduced me?'

Luis could feel the rage rolling beneath his skin. He'd wanted this opportunity to confront her with what she'd done, and back in Segovia it had all seemed so straightforward, so logical.

Without his parents there to intervene he would summon her, punish her, and then dismiss her.

Now that she was here, though, he wanted to teach her another kind of lesson completely. One that had nothing to with logic and reason and everything to do with lust. His eyes wandered over her beautiful face, dropping over her small rounded breasts to the temptingly smooth bare skin of her stomach. And as for dismissing her—

Breathing in sharply, he ignored the longing constricting his groin and dragged his gaze up to meet hers. 'Please don't treat me as though I'm stupid. Or naive. You'd be wrong on both counts. And you can stop all the wide-eyed outrage. I read your CV, Ms Shephard. I know exactly how your type operates and you set me up. All that business of spilling my drink…'

His mouth curled, contempt flaring in his eyes. 'I should have known something was up when you fixed my bike.' He shook his head. 'You only knew how to fix it because you'd broken it.'

And that expression on her face when she'd turned and looked back at him—it hadn't been doubt but relief. Relief that he was still there. His skin prickled with shame. Still there, fool that he had been, not struggling or fighting, just watching and waiting for her to reel him in.

Cristina stared at him in confusion. Her mind was completely empty, spotless—bare like a blank piece of paper. But it wasn't just his words that had robbed her of the power of thought. She just couldn't match the cold-eyed stranger in front of her with the man who had made love to her with such passion and intensity.

With an effort, she tried to marshal her brain into some kind of order. 'I don't know what you're talking about.'

Luis stared at her coldly. She was a good actress. *Really* good. The shaking hands were a particularly nice touch. He might have been tempted to believe her had he not been stung so badly before.

Five years ago he had been young, naive and insecure. The reporter back then had been older than him, pretty and persuasive, and he'd been flattered—

Until the moment when he'd woken up and heard her talking to her colleague.

His stomach quivered, dread pooling low down as he remembered how it had felt—not just the shock of discovering who she was, but the creeping recollection of what he'd said to her. Even now it still had the power to wake him some nights, sweating and yet cold, breathing heavily in the darkness.

A storm was building in his chest, and he knew his feelings must be showing on his face, but he didn't care. The proficiency of her performance only served to feed his anger.

'I told you not to treat me like an idiot. You might have fooled me once with those eyes, that mouth, but I learn from my mistakes—and *you* are a mistake I've no intention of repeating.'

Cristina felt familiar panic twist her stomach.

Meeting Luis with his parents had been a shock. But that had been all about his lies. This—here, now—was about his contempt. Her throat tightened, misery, dark and impenetrable, crowding out the breath in her lungs as his words ricocheted inside her head.

A mistake.

Suddenly it wasn't Luis's voice she could hear but her father's, and the words were those he had spoken to her eight years ago in a hotel foyer in London.

Her mouth felt bone-dry, and for a moment she thought she was going to throw up.

A week ago Luis had turned her body into a quivering mass of desire, his gaze, his touch, his kiss had made her feel as if she was the only woman in the world for him. Now, though, it was as if he could see inside her. See that she was a fake, a failure, with no place in the world—especially *his* world.

Watching the colour drain from her face, Luis felt something crack inside him.

She looked stunned—sick, even—and the fact that *he* was the one who had upset her made his heart beat painfully hard. He was never brutal— not even in business, and especially not to women.

But Cristina had lied to him. She'd let him believe that she wanted him, when all she'd really wanted had been to get the inside story on his family.

His mouth thinned. She didn't deserve gentleness or mercy.

He took a step closer. 'You lied to me. You knew who I was and you deliberately set out to seduce me. You followed me into that bar and then you made damn sure I noticed you. Hell, you even walked into me so that I'd spill my drink.'

That wasn't what had happened, she thought, striving to stay calm as a swirl of anger and frustration rose up inside her.

'Is that right, *Lucho*?' she snapped. 'You see, the way I remember it, you walked into *me*. Oh, and remind me again—which one of us was using a false name?'

Luis could barely contain his rage. It wasn't a false name. It was his childhood nickname. Even now his mother still used it sometimes, and Bas had always called him Lucho.

At the thought of his brother, the last thin thread of his temper snapped.

His eyes narrowed. 'You know, you're wasting

your talents, Ms Shephard. You should really be on the other side of the camera. Or is that what this is all really about? You selling some kiss and tell story to the newspapers?'

Cristina stepped forward, her hands curling into fists, frustration arrowing through her blood. 'For the last time—I didn't know who you were—'

'And I didn't know who *you* were.' His eyes met hers, dark grey with contempt and retribution. 'But I do now. I know exactly who and what you are. You're a cold-hearted, self-serving parasite.'

She could hardly breathe. 'And *you're* a phony. A fake. A fraud. Sneaking around, playing at being a biker, when really you're a CEO—'

'I was *not* sneaking.'

'Oh, really?' she snarled. 'Is that why your mother thought you flew in that morning? Why your father has no idea you ride a motorbike?'

A solid, choking anger filled his lungs. 'This is between you and I. It has nothing to do with my parents.'

'You're right. It did have nothing to do with your parents. Or my editor. It was just us.'

Just us.

The words spun out of her mouth, whirling between them like sparks—bright, luminous, impossible to ignore.

They were inches apart.

Luis could feel his body responding to her words, to the darkness of her pupils, to her mouth tipped up towards his—

Somewhere in the house a door slammed, and they both jumped.

Cristina stared past him, concentrating on the horizon. She felt weightless; as if the pulse beating between her thighs was all that remained of her body. It had been so hard not to reach out and touch him. But she hadn't, and soon he wouldn't be here to tempt her.

'And now it's over,' she said quickly, turning to face him. 'Look, I'm just here to work. So why don't you go back to California and let me get on with my job?'

Luis stared at her in silence. He was still reeling from what had just happened. His pulse shuddered. What had *nearly* just happened—and would have done if that door hadn't slammed, and brought him to his senses.

Senses that clearly needed to step up a level.

Stepping past her, he picked up the coffee pot and carefully filled two cups. 'Interesting hypothesis. But I'm not going back to California. Coffee?'

He held out a cup, and she shook her head. 'But you said—'

'Something I didn't mean, Ms Shephard. How

does it feel to be on the receiving end of that for once?'

His eyes locked onto hers.

'I don't trust you. I certainly don't trust you in *my* home with *my* parents. So while you're here I'm going to be here too. And every day I'm going to be watching you, waiting for you to mess up, and when you do I'm going to ruin you. But until that moment you're stuck with me.'

Staring past her, he gazed coolly at the sunset.

'You know your way out, don't you?'

CHAPTER FOUR

LEANING FORWARD, CRISTINA grabbed a handful of grass and hauled herself over a small outcrop of rock. The hill had looked quite gentle from a distance, but up close she had quickly realised that, like a lot things in life, its appearance was deceptive.

Scowling, she breathed out slowly.

It was yet another reason for her to loathe Luis Osorio, for she wouldn't even be up here if it wasn't for him. But after a restless night spent dissecting his remarks she had woken feeling just as tense and furious as when she'd gone to bed.

Back in London she would have distracted herself by going out and merging with the noise and the crowds, blending with friends and strangers at pubs and parties across the city, blanking out her brain with noise and laughter.

Only how could she do that stuck on a private island? There *were* no people or parties.

But there was no way she could just sit alone with her thoughts in that huge, beautiful bedroom, so she'd opted for her other go-to solution: exercise. After grabbing a bottle of water from the fridge, she'd headed towards the hill, expecting a walk and a view.

But of course nothing connected with Luis was what it seemed.

Her jaw tightened as his cool, hostile sound-bites replayed inside her head.

Out of all the men in that club, she'd had to go and sleep with him.

The sun was high in the sky now, but despite its heat a familiar damp clamminess was creeping over her skin. She felt numb. It would be easy to say it was just bad luck. That she was the victim of some massive cosmic conspiracy. That she had simply been in the wrong place at the wrong time.

But what would be the point?

She knew what had really happened. When he'd collided with her in the club it hadn't rendered her helpless or incapable of thought. The truth was that even before she'd felt the lean, hard muscles of his chest, or the power in his arms as he'd stopped her falling, she had wanted him.

Having sex with him had been her choice.

And his choice too.

She could feel the blood trembling beneath her skin.

Only he'd already distanced himself from that part of the equation. Distanced himself from her too. Just as her father had done.

Her father—

She felt a sting of pain in her chest. Why did everything always begin and end with her father? A man who thought so little of her that he had found it easy—effortless, really—to walk away. Nor had he felt any need to keep in touch. No letter telling her that he cared, no phone call to explain or justify his actions. Not so much as a backward glance. But then why *would* he look back? she thought dully. He already had a whole other life mapped out—another future—and it was easier to delete her and her mother, to rewrite history. Just as Luis had.

She shivered.

And that wasn't all they had in common.

Just like with her father, she had now given him the power to jeopardise her future.

Thinking back to what it had been like after her father had left, she took a breath, trying to steady the panic lurching in her stomach.

His desertion had, of course, devastated her thirteen-year-old self, but it had impacted on the future Cristina too. Angry and hurt, and with the cause of her anger and pain absent, she had turned on those who remained.

She had messed up her education, lost her friends, and lashed out at the one person who had consistently and unfailingly loved her—her mother.

It had taken years to get her life back on track,

and this photo shoot was her chance finally to be a part of something. Only now, just like always, she had managed to mess it up.

Her body stilled. It was awkward enough that she'd had sex with Luis—she couldn't even imagine what Grace would say if she found out—but there was also the matter of Luis wanting her gone.

Her insides tightened. Surely that wouldn't be up to him?

She bit her lip. Except that, like any normal parents, Agusto and Sofia were clearly devoted to their son. If he came up with a convincing enough excuse to end her contract it was inconceivable that they would take her side against him.

She felt her heart thud against her ribs. So the real question, then, was how far would he go to make good on his threat?

'That's great, Señor Osorio. If you could maybe lean in a little towards your wife. That's wonderful. Perhaps just a little bit closer. Wonderful.'

Cristina swallowed. At some point in the future she would look back to this day and see it as some sort of baptism of fire. A rite of passage that she might refer to in her memoirs. Right now, though, she just wanted it to be over.

She had probably taken hundreds, if not thousands of photographs over the last two years, but today nothing was working.

In theory it didn't matter. Today's shots were supposed to be 'fun'. Really they were just about making Agusto and Sofia feel comfortable around her, but instead they were making her question her ability to do the job.

She shivered on the inside. Maybe Grace's faith in her had been a little premature. Or, worse, could Luis's scathing remark about her experience actually be true?

Hating the way he had already managed to undermine her, she tried unsuccessfully to block his words from her head.

Only it was hard to do when the man himself was lounging negligently on a sofa to her left.

The sun was already high in a sky the colour of forget-me-nots, and both she and the Osorios were dressed for the heat—short sleeves, cool, pale fabrics. Luis, though, cut a sombre figure. Wearing a beautifully cut dark grey suit that made his eyes look almost black, a pale blue shirt and dark blue knitted tie, he looked as though he was about to preside over a full board meeting rather than sitting in on an informal photo shoot.

She felt a flicker of irritation.

His choice of clothing was obviously a deliberate attempt to sabotage the relaxed atmosphere she had been trying to create. And it didn't help either that he seemed determined to prove she was a scurrilous, manipulative hustler. Not only did he seem to be constantly there, policing her every move, he treated any attempt she made to engage him or his parents in conversation as some kind of an inquisition.

Aside from that he ignored her completely, immersing himself in his work so that she couldn't actually imagine him without his laptop.

Glancing furtively over to where he sat—one hand hovering over the keyboard, the other tracking a line of numbers on a paper printout—not for the first time she wondered how Luis 2.0 could be the same man who had stripped her naked and taken possession of her feverish body.

A memory of the earlier version of the man sitting opposite her dropped into her head—his mouth rough and urgent against hers, his eyes darkening as he lowered her onto the bed—and suddenly her mind went blank.

All she could think was how perfect it had felt…how perfect it had been.

When he'd banged into her in the club she had been blown away, knocked off her feet—not just literally but metaphorically. The attraction between them had been instant, inescapable.

She gritted her teeth. And now he was inescapable again, unfortunately…

Feeling completely exposed, she glanced back down at the camera, steadying herself. Then, staring at the photos, she felt her pulse start to accelerate. The composition and light were fine, but—

They said the camera never lied, and if that was true in this case her job had just got about a million times harder.

Agusto looked tense. Everything from the set of his shoulders to the tightness around his mouth suggested that he was not enjoying the photo shoot at all. But it was his wife's expression that made a knot form in Cristina's stomach.

Sofia was looking not at the camera but through it, her eyes focused on some distant point, as though she was searching for something that wasn't visible. She looked sad—hollowed out, almost.

Keeping her head bent over the camera, Cristina forced herself to click through the images on the screen, all the while making encouraging noises.

It wasn't just the sadness in the older woman's eyes that had caught her off guard, it was her own unintended intrusion into it.

Head spinning, she took a breath. She felt grubby, tainted. Just as she had when she'd caught that actress, with her philandering husband of three weeks, in a restaurant. Even now she could remember the thrill of it. She had thought being a *paparazza* was like being some kind of avenger.

A truth-chasing, justice-seeker on a bike, with a camera as her weapon of choice.

But watching that actress, who'd been younger than she herself was now, go into meltdown had made her feel physically sick. It could have made her a lot of money. It wasn't every day that an A-lister stripped down to her underwear in public. But instead it had been the reason she had quit chasing celebrities.

'Is there a problem?'

At the sound of the cool, clipped voice, she felt her fingers curl instinctively around the camera. Given his low opinion of her, Luis Osorio was the last person she wanted to talk to when she was feeling like a *paparazza* with his mother. But then he was pretty much the last person she wanted to talk to, or see, in *any* situation.

Although judging by the way her skin now felt as if it was on fire, it appeared that her body might have missed that particular memo.

Gritting her teeth, she trained an expression of what she hoped looked like serenity onto her face, and looked up at him.

At first, when she'd found him talking with his parents in the ornate sitting room the Osorios had chosen as a backdrop for the photos, she had assumed he would leave once she began to work. However, it had become clear almost immediately that he was keeping his promise to her. That not only was he going to watch her every move, but he was going to do so with an expression of utter contempt on his handsome face.

'Not at all,' she lied. 'It's all just part of the process.'

'Really? So all this playing with the light settings and changing lenses actually leads somewhere? That's good to know,' he said softly. 'To us amateurs it just looks like you don't know what you're doing.'

He held her gaze, and she felt her stomach tighten like a fist.

'By "amateurs" he means his mother and I,' Agusto said drily. 'Luis has a great interest in photography. He has quite a collection now.'

It was true. She had seen them around the fortress. His photographs ranged from Bauhaus Expressionism to nineteen-thirties social documentary, and were of a calibre normally not seen outside of galleries and museums.

Cristina kept her expression neutral. 'I know. I've noticed them.' She had admired them too, although no amount of waterboarding would have persuaded her to say so.

Turning, Sofia smiled fondly at her son. 'And he's met quite a number of the photographers personally—haven't you, *mi cariño*?'

Watching her son's face stiffen at the endearment, Cristina stifled a smile. But her amusement faded rapidly as Luis said slowly, 'I'm sure Ms Shephard doesn't want to hear about that now, Mamá. She is an artist at work, and we wouldn't want to interrupt her muse.'

For a moment she couldn't reply—she was too busy loathing the way he could say one thing and mean something entirely different. She knew definitively that he hadn't even looked at her work, and that he thought her 'muse' was Lady Luck.

Meeting his gaze, she felt her heart skip a beat as his dark grey eyes swept over her face.

'I'm happy for any interruption that includes an espresso, Señor Osorio,' she said sweetly.

Agusto laughed. 'I agree.' His earlier tension seemed to have shifted. 'Luis? Why don't you go and ask Pilar if she will bring us some coffee?'

'Isn't it a little early, Papá? It's barely ten o'clock.'

His father ignored him. 'And some of those *rosquillas* that she makes so well.'

Cristina held her breath as Luis stood up, his eyes steady on her face. If looks could kill, she might not be dead but she would be seriously maimed.

'I'll be right back,' he said stiffly.

Watching him stalk out of the room, Cristina released her breath. It was a relief to be free of his baleful presence—even it was only going to be a short respite. But she had no time to enjoy her small victory, as from inside her pocket she felt her phone vibrate. Normally she would never have answered it—particularly not with Luis looking for any opportunity to hint at her unprofession-alism—but it was the third time it had rung that morning, so it was probably someone from the office checking up on her.

'Excuse me, Señora Osorio. Would you mind if I took this call? It's the magazine.'

'Of course, my dear.' Sofia smiled. 'Agusto and I are just going to stretch our legs.'

Turning, Cristina walked quickly out of the room and swiped across the screen. 'Hello?'

'Hello? Is that Cristina? Cristina Shephard?'

The voice at the other end of the phone was a little breathless, as though the owner was ner-vous, or wasn't sure she was doing the right thing.

It didn't sound like anyone from the magazine, but then who else knew how to get hold of her? She had only just switched phones, and so far had only given her new number to the magazine, the Osorios and her mum.

Had something happened to her mother?

It seemed unlikely, but she couldn't stop the fear, sharp and irrational, spiking inside her.

'Hello, yes—who is this?' She flinched at the sound of her own voice. It sounded strange, taut and too high.

'You don't know me—well, you do, sort of…'

The woman hesitated. She sounded young—probably around her age—and in fact her voice sounded familiar. Cristina wondered why that should make her hand suddenly grow clammy against the phone—

'Only we've never met. I know you know about me, though, because you came to the hotel that time…' She hesitated again, and then gave a small, nervous laugh. 'I'm Laura.'

Laura.

It wasn't just the name that made her heart vibrate painfully inside her chest. Laura was a reminder of everything she'd lost and everything she'd failed to be.

Ice was slipping over her skin. It was lucky there was a wall behind her, she thought dazedly as she took a step back, pressing her spine against the cool plaster. Her legs felt like blades of grass and her mouth was dry.

The hotel.

Out of a lifetime of mistakes, that had probably been one of the worst.

And she wasn't about to repeat it now.

'I don't want to speak to you— I don't— I can't—'

'Please don't ha—'

She disconnected the call, her pulse racing. With trembling fingers she switched the phone to silent and stuffed it into her pocket.

Laura—

'Ms Shephard? Is there a problem? Not bad news, I hope?'

Cristina flinched. Hell—where had he come from?

For so many years she had imagined speaking to Laura. But not like this. And not now. Not with Luis Osorio staring at her, his dark gaze picking at the loose threads of her composure. He had already written her off, and she wasn't about to give him even more reason to despise and distrust her.

Forcing herself to meet his gaze, she shook her head. 'Sorry to disappoint you. It was just my editor,' she lied. 'I had a few ideas that I wanted to run past her.'

'Really? That's strange. I just got off the phone with her myself.'

Cristina swallowed. Of all the lies she could have picked, why had it been *that* one? And why did *he* have to be the one to catch her out in the lie?

The air between them was suddenly vibrating with tension.

'Actually, we got cut off,' she said quickly. 'I'll call her back later.'

Luis stared at her in silence. She had just lied to his face, and now she was doing it again. If she'd been cut off she would have looked irritated, or annoyed. But when he'd caught sight of her, slumped against the wall, the expression on her face had been not frustration but fear.

His pulse twitched. In fact she had looked distraught. So distraught that for a moment he had forgotten that she was the enemy. Forgotten that she couldn't be trusted. All he had wanted to do was reach out and— His brain paused. And what?

Hold her? Pull her close? Say something to wipe that look off her beautiful face?

He had been on the verge of doing it, but then she'd looked up at him and lied.

Just like that.

His anger simmered dangerously. How many times was she going to have to prove him right before he actually accepted the facts? That she had used him and that she was dangerous.

In two long strides he was in front of her, his arms on either side of her body, boxing her in against the wall.

'Don't take me for a fool, Ms Shephard. You might think that running with a pack of slobbering hyenas has made you tough. But you need to be *very* careful.'

His eyes locked with hers.

'I'm watching you. And the next time you lie to me will be the last.'

With the barest turn of his head, he pushed away from the wall and spun round.

'Pilar—let me take that tray.'

* * *

After lunch, Luis took a phone call of his own, and after he'd stepped out of the room Cristina felt her heartbeat return to normal again. It had been stupid to lie to him like that, for all she'd succeeded in doing was confirming his bad opinion of her.

But why did she care what Luis Osorio thought of her anyway? After this photo shoot she would never see him again. But for some reason she *did* care. Maybe it was because, just like her father, he found her wanting, and she so badly wanted to prove him wrong. Or maybe, after Laura's phone call, her defences had been down.

Either way, this was *not* the time to crumple.

She looked up and felt her heart contract. Agusto looked tired, but Sofia seemed drained.

'Señora Osorio, I was wondering…would it be possible to have a little look around the fortress? Just to get a feel of the place. I know how important it's been to your family.'

'Of course.' Sofia glanced at her husband. 'That would be fine—wouldn't it, Agusto?'

He nodded. 'Does that mean you don't want to take any more photographs today? Only…' his face softened as he looked at his wife '… I think Sofia and I could both do with a break.'

Cristina smiled. 'You deserve one. Most people find photo shoots exhausting and very stressful.'

'Pilar will be happy to show you around.' Sofia smiled.

'Or Luis could show you?' Agusto took a sip of his coffee. 'He knows all there is to know. He was even born here.'

'Oh, no, please—your son is a very busy man,' she said quickly. 'He doesn't need me interrupting his work.'

Her head was spinning. There was no way she was going to be stuck with Luis on her own.

Agusto shook his head. 'What my son needs is to realise that work isn't everything. That other things matter more.'

Catching sight of the pleading expression on his wife's face, he frowned.

'Just ignore me, Cristina. As usual, my wife is right. Pilar is the best person to show you around.'

Pilar would have made an excellent tour guide, Cristina thought an hour later. She was very knowledgeable, patient, and obviously passionate about her subject matter.

'So, did the family buy the island or the fortress first?'

'The island.'

They were climbing the steps to the tower. There were one hundred and twelve, which hadn't sounded like a lot until they'd reached just over halfway and the backs of Cristina's calves had started to burn.

'This is like a workout,' she said breathlessly on step ninety-one.

They finally reached the top.

'It is.' Pilar smiled. 'But you don't get this view with a normal workout.'

Turning slowly, Cristina gazed in silence at the view. 'It's incredible,' she murmured. 'You can see for miles.'

The housekeeper nodded. 'That's why the tower was built. To spot pirate ships.'

'Pirates? I thought they were from the Caribbean.'

Pilar laughed. 'Some were. But we had our own pirates here. From Africa. They were very determined, and ruthless. The fortress was built to keep them out.'

Cristina nodded. *Determined and ruthless.* Unprompted, a picture of Luis's beautiful, masculine face came into her head. Instantly she felt a tingling heat travel slowly over her skin, her body responding with indecent speed to the idea of Luis gazing out to sea, his grey eyes dark with predatory intent.

Yes, he would probably make a great pirate, she thought irritably. *And you would be the first person he'd make walk the plank.*

Downstairs were the family's private rooms.

'I don't need to see those,' Cristina said quickly.

'But you would like to see Baltasar's room.' It was a statement not a question.

Baltasar.

The son who had died in a car crash.

Grace had given her biographies of all the family members, but the information on Luis and his older brother had been basic—probably because her editor had believed it to be irrelevant for a photo shoot on Banco Osorio's four-hundredth anniversary.

Walking into the bedroom, Cristina realised that Grace had been wrong. Realised, too, why nothing had worked that morning. And why Agusto was so tense and Sofia so desolate.

There were many beautiful objects downstairs, but it what was missing that really mattered. Like negative space in a sketch, or silence in a piece of music, it told the hidden story.

In her house it had been her father's possessions. The shirts and suits left hanging in the wardrobe, never to be worn again. His precious vintage motorbike in the garage. And of course the letters addressed to him that kept on coming...

In Baltasar's room the shutters were half open and the room was cool and dark and quiet, and yet it seemed to hum with memories of the boy who'd lived there.

Her throat felt tight; the feelings she tried so hard to contain were swamping her. Her legs felt so rigid she thought they would snap—and then she saw it on the wall. A painting of two boys. Brothers. The older was smiling, clearly enjoying the attention. Loving it, in fact. And suddenly she found she was smiling too, for even on canvas his smile was infectious. He was blue-eyed, like his mother, and handsome. His grey-eyed younger brother seemed less at ease, more serious.

What held her gaze, though, was not the brothers but the gap between them. Or rather the lack of it. Turning, she gazed at the collection of photographs on a beautiful inlaid chest of drawers. Some were of the two boys, some included their parents—she frowned—and grandparents, maybe an aunt and uncle. But in each photo there was that same closeness.

Her earlier panic was fading. Maybe she would be able to take these photographs after all...

Sofia was sitting on the balcony, basking in the late-afternoon sun. Beside her Agusto dozed peacefully. Looking up, she smiled at Cristina. A book lay in her lap—a thriller that promised a 'breathtakingly brilliant and compulsive read'. But Cristina knew that it would be a miraculous book that could compete with Sofia's memories of her son.

'Was Pilar helpful?'

Striving for an appropriate level of enthusiasm, Cristina nodded eagerly.

'Yes, and I have an idea for the photographs. But...'

She hesitated. In her head, it seemed such a good idea. But what if she couldn't explain it properly? She had always been so bad at expressing herself—especially if it came to anything personal.

As though sensing the reason for her hesitation, Sofia patted the chair beside her. 'Start at the beginning. I find that usually works for me.'

Cristina felt some of the ache inside her chest ease.

'I was supposed to go to art college at eighteen, but I messed up.' Her mouth twisted. 'I was a bit of rebel at school, so I didn't end up going until a couple of years ago.'

Sofia nodded. 'That was a brave decision.'

Cristina shrugged. She hadn't felt brave. More like terrified. But she had wanted it so badly.

Glancing down at the cover of the book, she felt her heart start to race. Her need to learn, to improve, to be a good photographer had been compulsive.

She met Sofia's gentle blue eyes. 'I loved it,' she said simply. 'All of it except this one thing. We had to do a final project. The theme was "Legacy", and I couldn't make it work.'

Remembering her growing sense of panic, her hands tightened around the portfolio she was holding.

'Everything I tried felt fake. And then I was at home one afternoon and the post came, and there was a letter for my dad.' She hesitated. 'He was gone by then.' Gone was easier to say than left.

Sofia held her gaze, then nodded. 'And it inspired you?'

Cristina stared at her in silence.

In a way, yes. It had come almost nine years after he'd left. Nine years of silence—except that one time at the hotel, and then she had been the one doing the talking, or rather shouting.

They had probably moved six or seven times over those years. And yet there it had been, on the doormat. Her father's legacy to her—a letter from a clothing storage company, requesting payment for the two fur coats they had in cold storage.

She felt a tug on her heart. She hadn't shown her vegetarian mother the letter. But she had found inspiration for her project—a project that had been seen by Grace.

'Yes. It inspired me to take these photographs.' She held out the portfolio. 'I'd really like you to have a look at them.'

She sat with Sofia while she looked through the photographs.

Finally, the older woman closed the portfolio.

'Thank you, Cristina, for sharing these with me. I think I understand what you want to do, and I believe it will work beautifully.' Brushing a tear away from her cheek, she smiled. 'You're a very talented young woman, and your father would have been very proud of you.'

Cristina swallowed past the ache in her throat. Understandably, Sofia had thought that the photos were a memorial to her father. How could she reveal the truth?

That he had been a ghost in her life only this portfolio was not a record of his death but his absence.

That not only had he never been proud of her but he had judged her unworthy of his love and support.

She fixed a smile on her face.

'Thank you. I'll let you get back to your book.' She hesitated. 'If you don't mind, I'd like to photograph one of the paintings in your elder son's bedroom.'

For a moment Sofia didn't reply, and then, slowly, she nodded. 'Of course. And would you mind if I held on to this for a little longer?' Her mouth twitched. 'Like most men, Agusto responds so much better to show than tell.'

Upstairs, Cristina worked quickly. She felt excited—elated, almost—and desperate to explain her concept to the Osorios. Sofia, she was sure, would understand. Hopefully Agusto would too, and then—

'What the *hell* do you think you're doing?'

The voice was familiar, but the anger rippling through it exceeded anything she had ever experienced. Turning she felt alarm shiver down her spine.

Luis was more than angry. In the gloom of the room his features were almost luminous with fury.

She felt her whole body turn to stone, her mind blanking as his gaze locked onto the camera in her hand.

'I was just—' She croaked.

'Just what? Snooping? Stealing a little private shot?'

'No!' She shook her head, knowing exactly how it must look to him. But if knew the whole story... 'If you'd just let me speak—'

'You mean *lie*.'

'You're not giving me a chance—'

Luis stared at her in disbelief. 'A chance?' He repeated the word with distaste. 'I gave you a chance to prove me wrong. I let you stay. And look how well that turned out.'

'You just want to think the worst of me.'

There was a shaken note to her voice, but he told himself that he didn't care.

'And you make it almost pathetically easy for me to do so.'

Shivering, Cristina backed away. His voice was cold. But not as cold as his eyes.

'I can explain—' she began.

But her words dried to dust in her mouth as he strode across the room towards her.

'No—stop!'

She held up her hand but he just kept on walking, as though she hadn't even spoken.

'Please. Just let me explain.'

Her body bumped against the wall and she stopped moving. Her thoughts were racing. Had she imagined this situation she would have supposed that she would be scared. And she *was* scared—but not of him...not physically, anyway.

What scared her was the way he was looking at her—as though he'd seen who she really was. A boring, mousy little girl who didn't belong anywhere but especially not in his gilded world.

He stopped in front of her and the ferocity in his eyes sucked the breath from her lungs.

'You don't need to.' His lips were curling with contempt and the hostility of his gaze was giving her skin trauma. 'Your actions speak for themselves. I read your CV, remember? Once *paparazzi* always *paparazzi*.'

'No, you don't understand—'

It was the wrong thing to say. She knew that instantly as his expression hardened to stone.

'Oh, I understand. I understand that you're a leech. A parasite. You latch on to people and bleed them dry. Well, not this time. And not with my parents.'

Before she had a chance to register what he was doing his fingers had curled around her camera, tugged it out of her hand.

'First I'm going to wipe this clean—'

'You can't do that. It's my camera.'

And this is my home.' His eyes narrowed. 'And I want you gone from it. So first I'm going to wipe this clean, and then you're leaving—'

'That's not your decision to make.'

She made a grab for the camera but he held it out of reach, his other hand capturing hers. Then he jerked her against him.

'And yet I'm making it. So I suggest you lose that martyred expression or—'

'Or what?' She struggled against his grip, her fingers splaying ineffectually against the muscles of his chest. 'Oh, let me guess. This is where I get to choose between the hard way and the easy way?'

His grey eyes bored into her. 'You're wrong twice over. You don't get to choose. And there *is* no easy way.'

She jerked her hand free, her throat tightening.

'Oh, I know that. Believe me, I know there's no easy way. There never is.'

And before he had a chance to respond she ducked past him and walked swiftly out of the room.

Luis stared after her. For a moment he just stood there, too distracted by what she'd just said to follow. What did she mean about there never being an easy way? It made no sense.

Some of his anger began to fade. To be honest, he hadn't expected to get that angry with Cristina. Why would he? By nature he wasn't given to outbursts of emotion, but seeing her in Bas's room had been too much for him to handle and he'd lost his temper.

Only he hadn't meant to scare her—and he didn't like the feeling of knowing that he had.

His chest tightened and, turning, he stalked out of the room. He had to walk fast to catch up with her.

'Cristina—' he began.

'Oh, there you both are! I've been looking for you.'

It was his mother. He felt the familiar rush of guilt, and remorse as he watched her walk slowly towards them. He had broken her, and she would never recover. But as she got closer he saw that she was smiling.

'Mamá.You should have sent Pilar.' He frowned. 'Is there something wrong?'

His mother shook her head.

'Does something have to be wrong for a mother to look for her son?' Reaching out, she tapped the camera in his hand. 'I thought you liked buying photographs, not taking them.'

Luis glanced down. He had forgotten the camera. Had almost forgotten why he was holding it.

As a flare of frustration kicked up inside him he turned to Cristina, just as his mother said anxiously, '*Querida*, did you get what you wanted? It was the painting of Luis and Baltasar, wasn't it?'

He watched Cristina nod. 'Yes. Let me show you. May I?'

She held out her hand, and as he handed her the camera their eyes met. He knew that she wanted him to be a witness to the moment. Gazing down at the screen, he watched as she clicked through the photos right to the end, so that there could be no doubt as to what she'd taken.

Stepping forward, Sofia slid her arm through his. 'In that case I suggest we all go and have some *apéritifs* before supper. Agusto and I are dining out tonight,' she said, turning to Cristina. 'But don't worry—Luis has promised to take good care of you.'

Cristina smiled mechanically, but inside her

stomach plummeted. Given Luis's low opinion of her character, she was pretty sure that his version of 'taking care of her' was not going to be quite the same as his mother's.

Unless Sofia was also planning on dumping her into the sea at the first opportunity she had.

Dining alone with Luis would be the absolute last item on her bucket list, but there was no way she could get out of it, so at eight o'clock she found herself following Pilar out onto the terrace.

Luis had decided to eat outside, and it was difficult to find fault with his decision. The evening was warm, but not stuffy thanks to a faint breeze from the sea, and a vibrant orange sun was sinking below the horizon.

It was the most perfectly romantic setting she had ever seen. Or it would have been if the couple sitting at the table weren't more or less ignoring one another.

At least the food was heavenly, Cristina thought, swallowing a mouthful of the most delicious yellow *gazpacho* she had even eaten.

The soup was followed by lamb with smoked aubergines and then, for dessert, a *turrón* mousse. The wine was also delicious—a rich red Rioja with a streak of spice and blackberries—although she noticed that Luis stuck to water.

Perhaps he'd forgotten he was off-duty, she thought, her gaze drifting over his suit and tie—a mid-blue and stripe combination this time. She half expected him to hand her a memo, or start discussing the fiscal year.

In fact the absence of his laptop appeared to be his only concession to the informality of the occasion. Probably he wore a suit even when he went swimming. Or maybe he had a pair of pin-stripe swim shorts...

'Sorry—'

She felt sparks jolt over her skin as they both reached for the bottle of water at the same time and his fingers brushed against hers.

'Please—allow me,' he said, breaking the taut silence.

Her eyes locked onto his long, slim fingers, curling around the bottle, and she felt her heartbeat ripple. They'd curled around her waist in much the same way as she straddled him and he'd gazed up her, his grey eyes dark and intent.

She steadied her breathing as he filled her glass, then his. 'Thank you.'

'I'm just following orders.'

'That must make a change from giving them,' she said sweetly.

Luis held her gaze. 'I'm not a monster, Cristina.'

Even though he had acted like one earlier.

He gritted his teeth. Everything she did made him question himself. Each time he thought he'd got her all worked out she did something to throw him off balance, so that his behaviour over the last few days now seemed not reasonable but over the top and unnecessarily brutal.

It didn't help that whenever he was within her orbit his body kept overriding his brain and reminding him of just how perfectly she had fitted against him.

Breathing deeply, he forced himself to tune out his libido and concentrate on the here and now.

Tonight she looked poised and demure, in a cream blouse that showed off the pale golden skin of her arms and a pleated navy skirt that skimmed her knees. Her beauty was undeniable, but he wanted to see beneath the beauty.

Finding her in his brother's bedroom, he had been convinced of her guilt. Or maybe he had *wanted* to be convinced, he admitted a moment later. To make her fit into the category he'd assigned her: sexy but unscrupulous female photographer.

So maybe she had been right. He did want to think the worst of her.

But it was easier that way.

Easier than admitting to the facts.

That he couldn't stop thinking about her.

That even now part of his brain seemed intent on imagining all the different ways they could be making love on this table.

Heat rushed across his skin and he felt his muscles—*all* of them—tighten.

'Are those boats racing?'

Luis blinked as Cristina's voice broke into his heated thoughts and he turned towards where she was pointing. Out on the sea five small yachts, some with brightly coloured sails and fancy graphics, were chasing one another. It was a regular occurrence over the summer, and something he and his brother had frequently done using their own dinghy.

A memory of the excitement and the intensity of those races popped into his head and suddenly he was pushing his chair back and walking round the table to where the stone parapet edged the balcony.

Leaning forward, he gazed intently at the little boats. 'Yes, they are. It happens most weekends here in the summer. A bunch of local kids take their boats and race round the island. It's what me and my brother used to do when we were old enough to sail on our own. When were little we used to make bets on which boat would win.'

Cristina edged forward, drawn in by this sudden shift in conversation, and by the unexpected softness in his voice.

'How did you choose?'

She tensed as he turned towards her, fearing that she'd somehow spoilt the moment and that her casual question would be enough to make him retreat back into his anger and contempt.

But after a couple of seconds he shrugged. 'Bas just picked his favourite colours. So basically red or yellow sails, or best of all a combination of both.'

Taking a sip of her drink, she frowned. 'Why red and yellow?'

'They're our family colours.'

Remembering the crest on the side of the limousine, she gave a nod of understanding.

'Right—so what about you? I suppose you did some incredibly complicated mathematical equation to work out the odds?'

She stared at him curiously, but she wasn't really expecting him to reply. Judging by the way he was managing the conversation, the chances of him answering a direct question with a straight answer were remote to non-existent. Just like her father, he knew the risk of sharing too much personal information. It was safer by far to guide the conversation into more neutral territory, or better still talk about other people.

He held her gaze. 'Actually, I used to choose the shabbiest-looking boat.'

'You did?'

He nodded. 'I've always had a soft spot for the underdog.'

Her pulse twitched, and she felt a flush of colour warm her cheeks. Unsettled by the effect his words were having on her, she stared past him at the boats.

'So prove it.' The words tumbled out of her mouth before she could stop them. 'Pick a boat.'

He raised an eyebrow. 'Fine. The boat with the white sails is mine. You can have all the rest.' Taking a step forward, he held out his hand. 'Deal?'

It was more than a wager. It was a dare.

She shook his hand, almost forgetting to breathe as his warm fingers curled around hers. 'Deal.'

He tightened his grip. 'So, will you stop jumping to conclusions about me if I win?'

She lifted her chin. 'Only if you do the same with me. But let's just see what happens.'

To Cristina's amazement, Luis won.

'How did you know that would happen?'

Luis shrugged. 'Simple. Whoever's crewing that boat doesn't care about showy sails, just about sailing.'

'That's it?' She stared at him in disbelief.

Watching her eyes widen and soften, he felt a sudden rush of longing like a punch to the chest.

'Well, that and the way they were hugging the coast. It meant they didn't have to fight the winds when they got past the headland.'

His smile curved up, and Cristina breathed in sharply as it hooked her somewhere low in her stomach.

Unsmiling, Luis was stupidly handsome. But when he smiled his beauty was like the sun itself—impossible to ignore, mesmerising, dazzling. It made her forget his lies and his accusations.

She was still thinking about that smile when she excused herself to check her phone. After Laura's call she had been too scared to answer it, choosing instead to leave it on silent. But she'd checked her phone at various intervals in the day, and each time there had been several missed calls and messages from Laura.

Her hands trembled as she deleted the messages without listening to them.

She would deal with it when she was back home. Or maybe she wouldn't. All she knew was that she couldn't cope with it now.

She heard voices in the sitting room. Agusto and Sofia had returned, and from the snatches of conversation she concluded they had decided to have an after-dinner *digestif.*

She was just about to join them when she remembered that she'd forgotten to switch on the volume on her phone.

Stopping outside the door to the beautiful living room, she reached into her pocket just as she heard Sofia say quietly, 'I showed your father Cristina's photos—he thought they were wonderful. Did you look at them, Luis?

Body stilling, Cristina held her breath. She knew she should alert them to her presence—eavesdropping was wrong in so many ways—but her legs wouldn't move.

'Yes, Mamá, you know I did.'

Despite her nervousness, she couldn't help smiling. She liked the way Luis spoke to his mother. He was so gentle with her.

'I must have forgotten—'

'Well, I did.' She heard Luis sigh. 'And I know you don't want to hear it, but I haven't changed my mind. I think she's inexperienced and that shows in her work—which is competent but unremarkable.'

Cristina flinched, and then as the full impact of his words hit her the phone slipped from her hand. She watched it fall, her heart tumbling after it in her chest.

It wasn't just that he found her work lacking, it was that he had looked at her photos—personal photos that it had hurt her to take—and dismissed them as 'unremarkable'.

'But, Luis—' Sofia's voice.

'Mamá, we already discussed this, and I told you if having Cristina makes you happy then I'm happy to overlook her limitations.'

Her phone smashed onto the tiles.

Crouching down, she picked it up.

'Cristina?'

There was nowhere to hide. Standing up, she met Luis's gaze. It had been painful enough hearing her life, her talent, her hopes damned with such brutal precision, but watching Luis's face as he realised that she'd heard what he'd said was worse—for her humiliation was no longer just hers.

'I think I'm going to go to bed now—please say goodnight to your parents for me.'

And, turning, she walked blindly in the direction of her room.

But it didn't matter where she went, she realised as the tears began to roll down her cheeks. There was nowhere to hide from the truth.

She was a disappointment. A let-down. Easily dismissed and effortlessly forgotten.

CHAPTER FIVE

It SEEMED TO take for ever to get back to her bed-room.

Her legs wouldn't stop wobbling and she couldn't shake off the fear that Luis was going to come after her.

Not that there was any reason for him to do so, she thought dully as finally she reached the sanctuary of her room. He didn't like her. And now it appeared that he'd didn't respect her either.

Her stomach swayed.

Just like her father.

And she was so pathetic that she'd *still* let her head fill with fantasies of recreating that night they'd spent together. Still allowed herself to believe that there was something between them.

Her cheeks burned and, yanking open her wardrobe, she swiped at the tears filling the corners of her eyes. Well, now she knew the truth, she thought savagely, pulling out her suitcase.

Normally she hated packing. It reminded her too much of all the times she'd had to move home after her father had left, each time to somewhere smaller and more depressing and further away from the family life she'd taken for granted. Now, though, she didn't care. She just wanted to leave. To get as far away as possible from yet another man who had judged her and found her unsatisfactory.

Dumping her case on the bed, she began haphazardly stuffing clothes into it.

She had come here to turn her life around. To prove that she was worthy of recognition. That she deserved to belong.

Only once again she had been found lacking.

Her mouth trembled and she clamped it tighter.

So now what?

Stay and know that she was there not on the basis of merit but because the Osorios felt sorry for her?

No, thank you.

She was done with people feeling sorry for her. At school, her classmates' curiosity about her father's disappearance had been bad enough. But it had been her teachers' sympathy—the carefully worded letters home to her mother, offering counselling and access to the hardship fund—that she'd found almost impossible to endure.

Then she'd had no option. Aged thirteen, there had been no escape from their pity. But she wasn't a teenager now. She was an independent adult with freedom to make choices, and she was choosing to leave with some of her dignity intact.

Panic was prickling her skin. For years now she'd hidden her fears behind several coats of mascara and a couldn't-care-less pout. But now she could feel them all seeping out of her pores— for Luis had tapped into the worst fear of all. That once someone got beneath the surface and saw the real Cristina they would find her a disappointment, a failure, a fraud—

'Cristina.'

She hadn't heard him come in. She'd been too lost in the mental fog of her misery and anger. But it didn't matter anyway, for she had nothing to say to him.

'Cristina?'

He had crossed the room and was standing behind her.

She ignored him. No doubt his mother had sent him after her. What other reason could there be? From the moment she'd stepped on to the island Luis had made it perfectly clear that he didn't want her there.

'You can't just pretend I'm not here—'

No, she probably couldn't. But she wanted to.

Ever since her father had climbed into that taxi and simply not returned she'd felt abandoned, rejected. And yet for some reason she couldn't quite explain Luis's careless dismissal of her hurt more than anything else. Probably because it wasn't just her photographs he'd rejected. It was her and that night they'd spent together. That beautiful, extraordinary night they'd spent in Segovia.

A night when he'd renewed her faith in men and more importantly in herself. When he'd made her feel beautiful and extraordinary. Her mouth twisted. Only of course none of it had been real. He'd been acting, playing a part. Just as her father had liked to do.

And she'd fallen for it.

Just as her mother had done.

And just like her mother, even though she'd had no reason to trust him, she'd let her guard down again. Tonight she'd stood beside him in the fading light, trying to concentrate on the flotilla of little boats racing around the island. But when he'd turned that dark grey gaze to her, his eyes slowly unpicking the buttons on the front of her blouse, she'd forgotten all about the boats. Forgotten too about his lies and the vile accusations he made.

The urge to reach out and run her finger along the length of his jaw had been so strong, so sharp it had hurt.

Her breathing was suddenly staccato.

But not as much as it hurt now, to realise that it had all been in her head. That was what men like him did. They made you *feel*, they made you care about them, so that like some stupid moth you kept banging into the flame even though you knew that it would burn you.

She'd known all this and yet she'd still let herself believe that the way he looked at her, the way his hand brushed against hers, had meant something.

Gritting her teeth, she tossed a jumper into the suitcase—what a complete and utter fool!

A hand reached past her and flipped the suitcase shut.

'Will you stop for one moment?'

It was the first time she'd ever heard him raise his voice, and it was that as much as his sudden intervention that caused her finally to turn and face him, to change her misery into anger.

'Why? So you can gloat about me leaving?'

Luis stared at her, his dark eyes narrowing in on her face, and she let her gaze rest on his beautiful curving mouth and the clean-cut lines of his jaw and cheekbones until she could bear it no more.

'What are you talking about?'

'It's fine.' She held up her hand. 'We both know you never wanted me here in the first place—' she gestured towards the suitcase '—so you really don't have to pretend that you're sorry I'm leaving.'

'You can't leave.'

The expression on his face was difficult to

place. It should be relief—triumph, even—and yet it didn't look like either. Not that it mattered what he was feeling. It didn't change the fact that she wanted to get as far away as possible from him.

Slowly, she shook her head. 'There's a lot of things I can't do, Luis. Like algebra, and baking cakes, and apparently taking anything more than a "competent" photograph. But I can leave—and that's what I'm doing to do.'

Gritting his teeth, Luis watched as she turned back to the bed and began throwing more clothes into her suitcase. Despite the force and energy with which she was moving he could sense the numbness of despair spreading through her.

It was a numbness he knew only too well, for he had felt it too.

His mind looped back to the moment when he'd heard her phone smash to the floor. He'd known instantly that she'd heard his remark about her portfolio.

She might not have said as much, but the hurt expression on her face coupled with her swift, desperate retreat conveyed the truth as effectively as any words could have done.

And of course he'd felt bad—he had upset her, and he didn't like the way that made him feel. But he hadn't trusted himself enough to follow her.

Then he'd spoken to his mother.

His shoulders stiffened, and he closed his eyes.

What was it about Cristina that got under his skin?

For five years now his life had been orderly and meticulously planned. After his brother's death he had sworn never again to lose control. His days started with a workout and ended with sleep, and in between there was work. There were no spur-of-the-moment decisions, no acting on impulse.

Until Cristina.

And since then, for some reason, he'd ignored every rule he'd ever made, every instinct he had for self-preservation. From the moment he'd watched her walk past him in that square he'd been hooked.

At first he'd blamed his singular behaviour on his return. Even before he'd stepped onto the plane, he had known that coming back to Spain—to Segovia—was always going to be hard, unsettling, and sleeping with Cristina was surely demonstrative of that fact—one-night stands with sexy strangers were not his style and never had been.

Finding out she had deceived him—and, worse, that she had once been a *paparazza*—had been humiliating. But he had told himself that it was a testament to his unbalanced state of mind.

He'd arrived at the island confident that he

knew the 'real' Cristina—deceitful, unscrupulous, manipulative—and determined to expose her for what she was.

Only just when he'd thought he had proof—finding her snooping around his brother's bedroom—he'd had to revise his opinion of her. Not only had his mother given her permission to be there, but Cristina had been respectful and sensitive—not qualities he would have associated with the *paparazzi*.

His brain was still processing that thought as she slammed her suitcase shut.

Picking up the bag that held all her cameras, she swung round towards him. 'I'll go and say goodbye to your parents.'

'That won't be necessary,' he said quietly.

Her eyes widened with shock, and then her mouth curved into a contemptuous smile. 'Of course not. And you're right. You should be the one to tell them. You're so much better at twisting the facts than I am.'

Reaching down, he grabbed the suitcase from her hand and flung it on the bed.

'Nobody is telling my parents anything because there's no need. You're not leaving.'

Cristina stared at him. Her anger felt like a living thing, pulsing beneath her skin. She'd always known he was a control freak. Not just because of the way he'd insisted on overseeing the photo shoot, but because men like Luis and her father could only lead double lives by micro-managing every detail.

So, even though he'd wanted her to leave before she'd even arrived, it had to be on *his* terms.

Her face felt hot as she lifted her gaze to his face. 'Yes, I am.'

She didn't want to leave. But it was better that she went now. Better to leave with what was left of her pride intact, given that Luis's opinion wasn't about to change and any reprieve would only be temporary. If she left now maybe she might be able to persuade Grace that it had been her choice—for what was the alternative? Being made to feel like a hopeless fraud until someone—probably Grace—finally put her out of her misery?

'I'm going home.'

He stared at her intently. 'I thought you didn't have a home.'

She frowned, caught off guard by his words. How had he remembered what she'd said that night?

'I—I don't.' Her heart gave a jolt as she pictured her mother's rooms in the staff quarters where she worked. 'But I'd rather sleep on a park bench than stay here.'

Her voice sounded too high—and thin, as though it were about to fray—and she glanced away, furiously fighting the tears that were building in her throat.

'Please don't do that,' he said quietly. 'I don't want you to do that.'

'I don't care *what* you want,' she snapped.

Luis took a deep breath. His chest felt tight as his gaze dropped from her small, pale face to the bag she was holding in front of herself like a buffer between them. 'Do you care that I'm sorry?'

Watching the flicker of response in her caramel-coloured eyes, he felt his heart beat faster.

She shook her head. 'Sorry for what? Sorry that I heard what you said? Or sorry you didn't get a chance to prove to your parents what a worthless person I am?'

Something in her voice made his heart clench inside his chest. His hands curled involuntarily. Her pain sounded old, and he wondered where it came from. And why did it matter to him?

His eyes drifted over her face. He'd known beautiful women all his life. Some were so confident of their beauty that they expected to be fought over. But Cristina was different—exceptional, really. Her beauty was more than just an aesthetically pleasing arrangement of features. In part it was her vulnerability, in part her pride.

It was a pride he knew he had wounded—not intentionally but carelessly. Gazing at her, he felt his heartbeat accelerate as he saw the mix of doubt and defiance in her light brown eyes.

He took a breath. 'Please don't leave. I am sorry—sorry for what I said and for upsetting you.'

Cristina looked up at him warily. He sounded sincere, and with his dark eyes softer than she had ever seen them it would have been easy to accept his apology. Her stomach muscles clenched. But it didn't really change anything. He was apologising for his thoughtlessness, not his actual opinion, and it still hurt that he thought so little of her photographs.

'You're entitled to your point of view,' she said stiffly.

He stared at her pensively. 'No, I'm not.'

Before she could respond, he sighed.

'Whatever I said to my mother, I'm not entitled to any opinions on your photographs. Especially not these.'

He lifted his hand, and for the first time she registered that he was holding her portfolio.

She looked at him, her eyes wide and wary. 'You haven't looked at them.'

It wasn't a question but he shook his head anyway.

'No. I spoke to Grace, but I didn't look at any of your work.' He hesitated. 'Until just a moment ago.'

She head was suddenly swimming with fear, her hands clammy. She wanted to snatch the portfolio from his fingers, tear the photos into tiny shreds—anything but hear him try and pretend that he hadn't meant what he said.

'I don't care. I don't want to know—I don't need to know,' she said quickly, panic hoarsening her voice.

He held her gaze. 'They're incredible. And I know you'll think I'm probably just saying that, but I'm not. Your photos are more than "competent". They're poetic and powerful. You have real talent, Cristina,' he said simply.

There was a charged silence.

Cristina could feel the blood buzzing inside her head. She felt dizzy, and suddenly she was fighting to get on top of her emotions. For so long she had wanted to hear those words. To know that she mattered.

'You do believe me?'

To her surprise, he sounded anxious. She nodded slowly. 'Yes. I do.'

And she did. Maybe it was the hesitancy in his voice, or the way his eyes were fixed on hers, but somehow she knew that he was telling the truth.

He took a step towards her. 'Look, we made a deal tonight to stop jumping to conclusions about each other and I meant it.'

'I meant it too.'

'Good.' He breathed out. 'So, my mother said that you exhibited these?'

He was watching her closely, and she felt her pulse leap as their eyes met. God, he was so handsome. She'd been so busy hating him, hating herself, that she'd forgotten what it was like to be this close to him. Heat as dark and glossy as an oil slick slid over her as she remembered the last time they had been so close.

Pushing aside memories of that night, she cleared her throat. 'I did. That's how I met Grace, actually. She came to the exhibition.'

Her skin tightened with the same prickling excitement that she'd felt that day, when Grace had come over to her, casually held out a business card and told her to call her. It had only been later, sitting with her mother, trying to eat but still wound up with nerves and disbelief, that she'd realised Grace had written her personal mobile number on the back of the card.

Even now she still couldn't believe that she'd pulled it off—or that Grace was even real. But she was. And what was more she was the editor of the biggest news magazine in Europe. It was crazy. Meeting her had felt like one of those feel-good stories that got turned into films. She shivered. Except that in the movies her character wouldn't mess up her big break by having sex with the client's son.

Oh, yes, she would, she thought a moment later, as her eyes rested on Luis's handsome face. Unless for some reason she was trapped under a wardrobe during the entire film.

A very large and heavy wardrobe.

Dragging her gaze away from his beautiful, firm mouth, and the memory of what he could do with it, she forced herself to speak. 'She was kind to me. I didn't really have much experience...' Her cheeks felt warm, and she knew she was blushing. 'In portrait photography, I mean. But she gave me a chance.'

His dark eyes lingered on her face. 'Grace is smart and honest. And she's a very busy woman. If she gave you a chance it's because you deserved it. She must have seen something special in you...'

He paused, his gaze penetrating deep inside her, and then took a step closer.

'Just like I did.'

She felt her stomach lurch sideways in response to his simple statement. Nothing he'd said before had suggested that to be the case. Certainly there had been nothing in the way he'd behaved towards her to imply that he thought anything of her at all beyond his superficial and mistaken belief that she had shamelessly seduced him to further her career.

'What do you mean?'

Her eyes fluttered over his face. And as his

gaze locked onto hers her body stilled. She knew exactly what he meant, for even now she could still recall the intensity of his focus. And the way she had responded. There had been no boundaries between them. Even fully clothed she had felt naked.

As if he could see inside her head, Luis took another step closer, his dark grey gaze homing in on the pulse at the base of her throat, and her own eyes dropped to his mouth—that beautiful firm mouth—and instantly she was imagining how it would feel pressed against her bare skin.

Luis sucked in a breath. Around them the air was vibrating, tiny ripples of tension flaring out in waves. But what was he doing? He hadn't come here for this.

The blood was pounding in his veins, but somewhere deep inside his head he could hear a voice telling him to leave. To turn and walk away. Only for some reason he didn't move. It was as though his body was acting on instinct—like a boat slipping free of its moorings and following the swirling currents beneath the surface of the sea.

As if to prove that point he took another step closer, and now he was close enough to feel the heat of her skin like a caress.

'I mean this,' he said softly and, leaning forward, touched his mouth to hers lightly.

He felt a jolt like lightning—felt his breath spinning out of him at the softness of her lips—and the intensity of his desire almost knocked him off his feet.

With an effort he lifted his head, and as her eyes collided with his they stared at one another in the pulsing silence.

Cristina felt dizzy. Not the fainting, falling over kind. The kind you got when you went on the Waltzer at the funfair. A tingling, shivering rush of endorphins that mixed fear with excitement and pleasure.

She didn't want to feel like this. Deep down she knew that she should be fighting it. But whatever logic and common sense arguments she should have in her head had been eclipsed the moment his lips had touched hers.

Her heart seemed to slide sideways. She could still feel Luis's gaze, his dark grey eyes seeking her out, impossible to ignore, futile to resist.

She turned towards him, her breath hot and scratchy in her throat. He held her gaze and then slowly lowered his mouth back to hers, kissed her again.

Cristina moaned as heat exploded inside her. Her lips parted and she was kissing him back, her hands seeking out the warm muscles of his arms, her fingers curling into the fabric of her shirt.

It would have been a lie to say that she had forgotten what it felt like to be kissed by him. She hadn't. She'd dreamed about it so often and so intensely that some mornings she'd woken and reached across the bed to find him. But she saw now that no dream could match the reality of Luis's warm, firm body against hers.

She shook with need as he opened her lips, deepening the kiss, his mouth claiming hers, his hand curving around her waist and pressing her against the hard breadth of his chest. And then his fingers splayed against her back, anchoring her closer, and he was tipping her head, kissing down her neck.

Her stomach tensed and she squirmed against him, wanting more, feeling the pulse beneath her skin and between her legs urgent now.

As though reading her thoughts, Luis tightened his hands around her waist and in her hair, and then they were stumbling backwards towards her bed.

Panting, she pulled him closer, her fingers curling into his belt, clumsily plucking at the buckle. His low groan made her legs start to shake.

Breathing unevenly, he dropped the portfolio on the table by the bed and began pulling at the buttons on her blouse. She felt cool air on her skin and, whimpering, let her head fall back, her eyes seeking something solid to combat the dizzying effect of the heat soaking her skin.

She blinked. Her portfolio was lying on the table, where he'd dropped it, but some of the photos had fallen to the floor. Her heartbeat slowing, she stared at them dazedly.

Suddenly her breath felt like concrete in her chest. She wanted to look away but she couldn't. Her eyes wouldn't let her.

Maybe if it had been another photo... But how could she expect to block that image out?

She stared miserably at the photograph. That briefcase had changed her life. Or rather opening it had. Had totally destroyed everything she had believed to be true. Two letters and a snapshot had been all it took to stop her world from turning.

Her body must have frozen, for she felt Luis grow still against her and she breathed in sharply, her hands shrinking back from his body.

Where moments earlier there had been sweet pulsing heat, now panic was rising inside her.

What the hell had she been thinking?

Had she really been going to have sex with Luis again?

Last time had been stupid, but forgivable. She hadn't known his real identity. Or that he was happy to lie about who he was. But she had known the truth since the moment he had walked into his parents' sitting room.

Briefly she closed her eyes. So either she was

stupid or she was genetically determined to follow the disastrous path her mother had taken. Either way, the outcome would be the same. Pain, humiliation, rejection.

'Cristina—'

The urgency in his voice cut into her thoughts and, gazing up at him, she took a shaky step backwards. 'This is wrong.'

Luis stared at her in confusion. Wrong? *Wrong?* What did she mean? Her words didn't seem compatible with the painfully aroused state of his body.

Somewhere inside what was currently functioning as his brain, he tried to make sense of what she'd said.

'Ah, you're not protected?' He frowned. 'I have condoms in my room...'

Cristina felt heat spread over her face. She had been so frantic, so lost in her own responses, that she hadn't even considered whether she was protected or not. That had *never* happened—ever—and it was one more reason why this had to stop. Now.

She shook her head, trying to focus on something other than his handsome face. It didn't help that her longing for him was still clawing inside her like a frightened animal.

'No, it's not that. It's this—us. We shouldn't be doing this—'

Because…?' he said slowly.

She stared at him blankly. What was she supposed to say? The truth? That she don't want to become her mother. Or be with a man like her father. That she didn't want to get hurt and that although having sex with him would be incredible it would also ruin her life—the life she'd only just got back.

Her throat felt tight with panic.

No, she couldn't tell him the truth, for that would mean revealing more about herself than she had ever shared with anyone.

'Because I don't want it. I don't want *you*.'

An ache was building in her chest. She wanted to change her mind. To rewind back to the moment before she saw that photo and to close her eyes. But it was too late.

'But I thought—' he began.

'Then you thought wrong,' she said curtly, wincing inside as she spoke. 'I don't want you here and I'd like you to leave. Please.'

She watched his face twist, harden.

'You don't want me?'

He said it slowly, as if he didn't believe her, and judging by the look on his face he didn't. For that she could hardly blame him. She didn't believe herself either.

'So this…' He gestured towards his unbuckled belt. 'This was you not wanting me?'

She cleared her throat. 'You misunderstand me.'

Her voice sounded too clear, and too high, but she didn't care. She just wanted to get the words out so that he would leave before she fell to pieces.

'I do want you—but only because you're here.'

He took a deep breath. 'Is that right?'

Words failed her and she nodded. Suddenly she was hanging on by a thread. 'Yes. I'm sorry.'

But her apology went unheard. Before she had even finished speaking he had turned and stalked out of the room, closing the door softly behind him.

She collapsed onto the bed.

Some men would have lost their temper. One or two might even have ignored her protests and carried on. Most of them would have slammed the door.

But not Luis.

Her eyes were burning. People said that the truth hurt. And it did. Only nobody ever said that lying hurt more. Worse, she clearly had a natural propensity for deceit, so that after years of believing she was her mother's child it turned out that she was actually more like her father.

Overwhelmed with confusion, and misery, she fell back against the pillow, and began to cry softly.

CHAPTER SIX

STRIDING INTO HIS BEDROOM, Luis resisted the urge to slam the door and instead began pacing frenetically across the floor. He felt as if he'd been hit by a truck. He could see his body and yet it seemed unconnected to his brain. Or rather the mass of tumbling, incoherent blink-and-you'd-miss-them thoughts that appeared to be all that remained of his brain.

What the hell had he been *thinking*?

Glancing down at the hard outline of his erection pressing against his trousers, he gritted his teeth. Not much, apparently. Or at least nothing that had anything to do with logic or common sense. His entire being had been focused on the need to take Cristina in his arms.

And not just for some hot, feverish kisses either.

The truth was that he had wanted her in the most basic, primitive way. Needed her in the same way that a starving dog needed a bone.

He started pacing again, his footsteps matching the thumping of his heart. It had been just like that night in Segovia—only this time the storm had been beneath his skin, a whirlwind of heat and desire, spinning out of control, whipping his senses until he'd had no choice but to reach out to her.

His chest was burning and he realised that he'd been holding his breath, his rapt body caught up in how it had felt to touch Cristina again, to lose himself in the sweetness of her kiss.

Remembering how she'd pushed him away, and the distance in her voice as she'd told him that she only wanted him because he was there, he felt his stomach clench. Not with anger—for that would have meant he thought she was telling the truth, and he knew without question that she had been lying to him.

Except, of course, the part when she'd told him that she wanted him to leave. She *had* wanted him to leave, but only because she didn't want a witness to her pain. A week ago he would have believed her cover story—would have been drawn by the apparent confirmation in her words of who he thought she was: a hustler he had every reason not to trust.

Now, though, it wasn't Cristina he was struggling to trust but himself.

An image of her face—pale, strained and young—slid into his head, and he felt his breathing quicken. Suddenly he was moving again, as though by doing so he could put some space between himself and that picture of her looking so tense and wary.

Had she wanted to, she could easily have seduced him. It would have been the perfect moment, for there was no way he could have resisted her. She had brought him to his knees…reduced him to nothing more than a rippling mass of impulses. His face felt suddenly hot with an almost adolescent shame as he remembered how effortlessly she had robbed him of his reason and resistance.

But hadn't it been inevitable that it should happen? They'd been alone in her room, and they'd been tiptoeing around one another since the moment she'd stepped foot on the island, the attraction between them invisible and yet omnipresent, heavy and taut—like rain about to fall.

So why, then, had she stopped?

A beat of blood pulsed inside his chest.

Every time he'd imagined just such a scenario in his head it had played out in many ways, but each time the outcome had been the same. With the two of them alone in her room, Cristina lifting her mouth to his, her breath whispering against his lips, her body blurring beneath his fingers…

He'd expected her to offer herself to him, slowly peeling off her clothes in front of his unfocused gaze, only for him to push her away, demonstrating his resolve before casually turning his back on her.

Only none of that had happened. It had been she who had stopped it—not him. He'd been wrong, so maybe he'd been wrong about her in Segovia. Maybe she really *hadn't* known who he was.

His mouth twisted.

Or maybe she was playing the long game? Using her body to mess with his head.

How was he supposed to know?

He'd thought he understood Cristina but he didn't know the woman who had pushed him away, and her sudden physical and emotional retreat was not just baffling, it had got under his skin.

It was all deeply unsatisfactory. And confusing. And he hated it. He disliked and distrusted anything he couldn't classify and contain. But it was proving impossible to do either with Cristina, or any decision involving her.

Even his presence on the island now seemed rash and irrational; he was there because he'd thought she had set him up and he didn't trust her to be near his parents. Now, though, that image of an unscrupulous, manipulative Cristina just didn't match up with the panicked woman he had watched retreat into herself. He no longer knew what was real and what was just him being paranoid.

What he did know was that being around her all the time was no longer necessary on his parents' account. If she was a threat to anything it was to his sanity and—he glanced down at the outline of his erection—to his self-control.

He couldn't function with Cristina constantly in his thoughts. And she *was* in his thoughts all the time—at breakfast, during every single lap he swam in the pool, and as he was lying wide-eyed in his bed every night.

He needed distance and discipline. Not easy when he was stuck here with a woman who could so easily bypass his defences. The only woman, in fact, ever to do so.

His lip curled. The less time he spent with her the better—and not just because his physical response to her was instant, extreme, and quite frankly painful. She threatened his equilibrium in other ways. Feeling her withdraw from him, watching that flicker of vulnerability in those beautiful brown eyes, had moved him more than he was willing to acknowledge.

He blew out a breath. Cristina had got inside his head and she was proving impossible to dislodge. But there was a solution—an obvious one. Work had never let him down, and in having decided to stay in Spain he had created an ample backlog for himself. He would speak to his PA and soon he would be too busy to think about Cristina Shephard.

For now though, a cold shower should help dull

the ache in his groin and, turning, he walked determinedly towards the bathroom.

On legs that still shook Cristina walked across the room and closed her window. She knew logically that it wasn't cold. She could see the sun and feel the warm air on her skin. But that didn't seem to matter. She felt cold to the bone and brutally tired—as though she'd run a race.

Her mouth trembled. A race she'd clearly lost.

Maybe it would always be like this. Maybe it wouldn't matter how fast or how far she ran she would never escape her past. Somehow it would always pull her back.

Reaching down, she picked up the photographs from where they'd fallen. She carefully pushed them back into the portfolio and sat down on the bed.

It was her own fault. She should have told him to leave sooner. Or better still left herself.

She shivered, a pulse of fear and longing beating beneath her skin. But how could she have done either?

Being so close to him had rendered her not just incapable of speech—it had deprived her of any sense of self-preservation. Why else had she acted so recklessly? Letting him kiss her like that and then kissing him back...

Remembering the feel of Luis's mouth and

hands on her body, she breathed in sharply, a ball of heat rolling over inside her. Despite suggesting that she had only wanted him because he was there, the truth was that she had been prepared to risk *everything*—including her future—in order to satisfy her desperate need for him.

And if she hadn't caught sight of that photograph—

Her breathing stalled in her throat.

It she hadn't come to her senses, then what?

Would she have gone all the way?

Her mouth slanted upwards in a not-quite smile. *All the way.* She sounded like a teenager. Her smile faded. Except that your average teenager was actually pretty savvy and switched on, whereas *she* had been like a leaf tossed in the wind, with desire driving her actions, not just disregarding the consequences but failing even to acknowledge them.

How could she have been so stupid? So short-sighted?

She steadied her breathing.

But she wasn't completely to blame. If Luis hadn't come to her room—

Her throat started to prickle. She knew she was overly sensitive, and she despised herself for caring about other people's opinions—particularly his—but it had hurt hearing him dismiss her portfolio like that. Only then he'd come to find her, and apologised, and then—

Her thoughts were running away from her like meltwater in the spring. With an effort, she slowed her breathing again.

It was his gentleness that had messed with her head. Coming so soon after he'd been so cold and cutting, it had caught her off balance and broken down the walls she'd built around herself. He had made her feel as though he cared, that she could trust him.

Trust.

Her mind snagged on the word.

Luis couldn't be trusted. She knew that. The cool-eyed biker she had met in that club was the antithesis of the sober, suit-wearing heir to the Osorio fortune—and who knew how many other versions of him there were?

She'd learned from her father that living more than one life was an addiction that overrode everything—family, finances, even the laws of physics—for how else had he managed to be in two places at once?

Her mouth twisted. All of which meant that she could never trust Luis. Oh, she'd thought he was different once. In Segovia she'd believed that he was gritty and real, but she knew now that he was just like her father—all stubble and no soul.

Yes, he wanted her—but only in the way that she'd claimed to have wanted him, because she was there. No doubt he would distance himself as soon as he found something more interesting.

Slowly Cristina stood up and pulled her suitcase across the bed. There was nothing to be gained from picking over everything again and again. If she was going to stay—and she was—then she needed to focus, not waste time or energy wanting something from him that in reality couldn't ever exist.

The next day she was relieved to discover that Luis was not at breakfast. She would have faced him, of course, but even thinking about seeing him again made her skin feel hot and tight. Thankfully, the photo shoot was finally going well, and the glow of everything coming together absorbed her all morning.

There were many reminders of Baltasar around the house, but in the end Agusto had chosen a yachting medal and Sofia her son's favourite book. Their choices were not just proof of his life, they were charged with a deep, unwavering love, and perfectly captured both Bas's unalterable absence and his continued presence in his family's life.

Of course the living were harder to forget, and as the morning lengthened Luis was still absent. From feeling grateful that he was no longer watching her every move, some of her elation started to ooze away. In fact by lunchtime his absence was making her feel on edge in the same way that his presence once had.

Glancing at the table, she felt almost light-headed as she saw that it was set for three. 'Is Luis not joining us?'

The question was out of her mouth before her brain had a chance to censor it.

She steeled herself as Sofia looked up at her, praying that her expression showed no trace of any intimacy between herself and the older woman's son.

'No, *querida*. He's popped over to the mainland. Something to do with business. He'll be away for a couple of days.' Looking across to where her husband was talking to Pilar, Sofia lowered her voice. 'He works so hard. Too hard, we think. But...'

She shrugged—a wordless gesture that somehow managed to imply both regret and confusion.

Cristina swallowed. She had grown fond of the older woman, and hated seeing her look so sad. Forcing brightness into her voice, she said quickly, 'It's not that surprising, is it? Your husband is still working now. Probably he worked even harder when he was younger.'

Sofia gave her a small, tight smile. 'He did. But it was different. Agusto was different.' She sighed. 'He worked for his family and to remind himself of his heritage.' Her smile stiffened. 'Luis works to *forget* that heritage.'

But why?

The question formed on Cristina's lips, but just as she opened her mouth to ask it Agusto turned towards them and the conversation moved on to the options for dessert.

The next day followed the same pattern—work interspersed with periods of trying not to think about Luis. Mealtimes were the worst, and despite enjoying spending time with Agusto and Sofia, she missed him so much that it hurt like a bruise just above her heart. Not that her heart was actually involved in their particular dynamic. Probably the ache was just a phantom memory— a reminder of how she had felt when her father had left.

As usual, thinking about her father made the breath rattle in her throat, and with a pure effort of will she forced herself to blank all thoughts other than work from her mind.

At first it worked.

She spent the afternoon playing around with the photos on her laptop, but her focus of a few days earlier had evaporated. The screen might as well have been blank for all the attention she gave it. Instead she couldn't stop thinking about what Sofia had said about her son, and her sadness. Her words played inside Cristina's head as images of Luis looped through her mind. His dark eyes as she'd asked him to leave, that blank look on his face the moment before he'd turned and walked out…

Her downshifting mood and diminishing concentration weren't helped by her phone vibrating with persistent regularity in her pocket.

Finally, it was time to wander up to the main house for supper.

She hadn't been expecting to see Luis, but even so the sight of the table once again set only for three gave her a jolt. The meal seemed to last for ever, and by the end her face was aching with the effort of smiling. Finally, pleading tiredness and a need for an early night, she excused herself and, back in her room, she lay down on her bed, willing herself to fall asleep.

It didn't work.

Her body felt impossibly restless. There was a sharpness beneath her ribs, and her breathing faltered in her chest. And she knew why she was feeling like this now. It was because he wasn't here.

She was missing him.

Rolling onto her back, she gazed up at the ceiling in confusion.

That made no sense at all. For the last few days

she'd been desperate to escape his cool, critical gaze, so why should she be missing him now?

She should be celebrating, or at least feeling grateful that she wasn't having to spend time with him, for it was clear that despite praising her photos he still thought she was shallow, devious and not to be trusted. His barely concealed contempt for her had left her as breathless as his lovemaking.

Her pulse gave a twitch, heat flaring inside her as she remembered how Luis made love. The cool touch of his fingers, the heat of his mouth, the hard thrust of his body against hers, the feeling that when finally he pulled away she had lost a part of herself...

Her phone vibrated on the bed beside her and her body froze, her thoughts abruptly eclipsed by a shifting and by now familiar apprehension. Glancing down, she felt almost winded with relief as she saw it was her mother calling.

'Hi, Mum.'

Pressing the phone against the side of her face, a rush of homesickness hit her head-on as she pictured her mother in her room.

'Oh, Chrissie—thank goodness.'

Hearing the agitation in her mother's voice, Cristina felt suddenly nauseous. Her mum was usually so good at hiding her emotions, but she wasn't even trying.

'What's the matter?'

Her heart seemed to drop inside her chest. Could Laura have contacted her mother? It seemed unlikely, but not impossible.

Trying to keep her voice steady, she said, 'Has something happened?'

'I've been leaving you messages for days. I thought something had happened to you. I know it's late, and I wasn't going to ring, but I couldn't bear it—'

Her mother's voice wobbled and Cristina gripped the phone more tightly, guilt coursing through her. After her father had left both she and her mother had become scrupulous about staying in touch. Even when she'd been at her worst— bunking off school, staying out all night—she'd still called her mum and answered every text from her.

'I'm *so* sorry, Mum.' She spoke quickly, desperate to reassure the one person in her life who had been constant and caring. 'The signal here isn't great,' she lied. 'And my phone keeps losing charge.' Another lie. 'It's been a crazy few days.' That was true—although not in the way she was making it sound.

The rest of the conversation was much easier. Her mum was a good listener, and so partisan in support of her daughter that Cristina found herself relaxing for the first time in days. But even as she said goodbye she could feel her earlier tension returning.

Gritting her teeth, she gave up all thoughts of an early night and, standing up, unzipped her dress and let it fall to the floor.

Ten minutes later, with a full moon above her, she was running along the cliff path, a light breeze in her face. Usually in London she wore headphones, to block out the noise of the traffic, but here there was no need. It was the first time she'd run in weeks, and the absence of any noise and the taste of clean air and sea spray was as exhilarating as neat alcohol.

Slowing down slightly, she zig-zagged through a clump of pine trees down towards the beach, her gaze following the pale path beneath her feet. And then she was on the beach, her trainers sinking into damp sand and the sound of the surf filling her head.

Hands on her hips, she breathed out slowly, enjoying the relentless motion of the waves and the sheer, dizzying pleasure of being so close the sea. She looked longingly down at the water. It would be so lovely to go for a quick swim. But then again…

She sighed. Swimming alone at night in a sea she didn't know was probably not the most sensible idea. Maybe she'd get up early and come back tomorrow—

Glancing up the beach, she stopped mid-thought, her attention snagged by a movement on the dark rocks—a flash of white.

Was it a bird?

Frowning, she walked swiftly across the sand. Up close, the rocks were slightly steeper than she'd anticipated, but she managed to grapple her way to the top. It was higher up than she had thought, but on the plus side she could see that there was a less arduous way back through the pine trees.

For a second she gazed at the path, mentally tracing it up the hill. Heart still pounding, she made her way cautiously over the rocks—and then abruptly stopped.

Gazing down, she felt a tug of excitement. It was a tidal pool, almost circular, maybe ten metres wide, carved out and fed by the sea and perfectly hidden. Pulse twitching, she watched the waves lap over the edge of the rocks—and then, without warning, her breath caught in her throat and she took a step back.

Beneath her, swimming with smooth, effortless grace was Luis.

He was on his front, wearing nothing except a pair of blue swimming shorts with a flash of white. Feeling like a voyeur, but unable to stop herself, she inched forward, her eyes locked on his muscular back and the smooth, sleek lines of his limbs.

She knew she should move, but her feet seemed to be embedded in the rock beneath her. All she could do—all she wanted to do—was stare. And then, just like that, he was pulling himself out onto a terrace of rock, smoothing his hand over his wet hair, and it was too late for her to do anything.

Pulse soaring, she watched mesmerised as he made his way up towards where she standing. Right at the last moment he looked up and froze.

Cristina stared at him mutely, her skin on fire as though the moonlight was burning her. Sea water was trickling down from his shoulders over his chest and stomach, and his eyes were deeper and darker than the pool behind him. He looked like some mythological hero. Her gaze dipped to his mouth. But he was real.

Luis felt his muscles contract.

What the hell was she doing here?

He'd thought he was alone, and judging by her next remark Cristina had clearly been thinking the same thing.'

'I didn't know you were here. I thought you were on the mainland.'

Blood singing in his ears, Luis stared at her dumbly. Having made up his mind after their catastrophic kiss not to spend any more time with her than necessary, he had been avoiding her masterfully—even going to the trouble of arranging a meeting with a business colleague on the mainland.

His mouth tightened. *If it wasn't so tragic it might almost be funny!*

He'd gone away ostensibly to work, in reality to forget her. But he'd done neither.

Her name, her face, her body, even her voice had been impossible to forget, for she was inside his head. He could taste her in his mouth, feel her swimming through his blood just as he had swum across the pool.

And it wasn't just his memory and his body that seemed determined to remind him of her at every opportunity. The flowers on the table had conspired against him too, their scent reminding him of her and causing him to lose track of what he was saying on more than one occasion during lunch.

He gritted his teeth. He'd tried to stay away, but he couldn't. His need to see her, to be near her, kept pulling deep inside him, strong and relentless, like a marlin on the end of a line. And even though he'd known that returning to the island was an admission of weakness he'd come back anyway.

But seeing her like this, *here*—

His breath felt suddenly too low in his chest. This place was almost sacred to him. Bas had taught him to dive here. They'd tried their first and only cigarette sitting on these rocks. And it was where they'd always come to trade their fears and hopes.

Now he was here with Cristina. A woman he didn't fully trust and yet who reminded him so much of his brother—not just in her beauty but in her effortless rapport with people even his parents. Usually they were quite formal and reserved with anyone except immediate family and longstanding friends, but they were both already clearly fond of Cristina, and she was delightful with them.

He might have been—*would* have been—suspicious of her motives had she only bothered to sweet-talk Sofia and Agusto, but he'd watched her with Pilar and with Gregorio, the estate's elderly and quite deaf groundsman, and she behaved with exactly the same easy empathy.

Behind him a wave splashed loudly against the rocks and, aware suddenly of his own stillness and silence, he cleared his throat. 'I decided to come back early...'

He hesitated. Having started to speak he now realised that not only did he not have a reason for coming back ahead of schedule—or at least not one he was prepared to share with Cristina—he also hadn't considered the possible interpretations of his change of heart.

'I was planning on meeting with some potential investors tomorrow, only my team are still working on the pitchbook so—'

He broke off as Cristina looked up at him blankly. 'What's a pitchbook?'

'A pitchbook is a presentation we give to investors. It outlines the firm's strategy, its principles, performance and terms of investment.'

'Oh, I see.'

Watching her nod slowly, he gritted his teeth. For some reason he wished that they hadn't started talking about work. Maybe it was because he was wearing swimming shorts, not his suit, or perhaps it was just that—weirdly—it didn't seem that important right now. Either way, he knew that he wanted to make it clear to her that his life wasn't all meetings and memos.

His eyes met hers. 'And, of course, I wanted a swim.'

'You did?' Her chin jerked up, brown eyes widening with surprise.

'Is that such a shock?'

He held her gaze, and it was as if a pulse beat in the air between them.

Cristina blinked. 'Well, yes…kind of. I mean, I haven't seen you out of a suit since I arrived. I just thought maybe you didn't *do* beaches or swimming or getting wet.'

She glanced furtively at the line of fine dark

hair disappearing into his shorts, trying not to remember what lay beneath.

'I got pretty wet in Segovia,' he said quietly. 'Or have you forgotten?'

No, she hadn't forgotten. Remembering how he'd stripped off his sodden T-shirt in her bedroom, she felt her pulse began to beat out of time.

Shaking her head, she waited for her heart to slow before she replied. 'Not at all.'

A warm breeze was catching the ends of her hair and grateful for the chance to distract herself—and him—from the conversation, she ducked her head.

Grabbing the wayward curls, she said, as casually as she could manage, 'I'm sorry for interrupting your swim. I just needed a run, and... Anyway, I'll get out of your way—'

For a moment she thought he was simply going to nod and walk back to the pool, but instead he stared at her in silence, his grey eyes fixed on her face.

'Why did you need a run?' he said finally.

Her throat tightened.

Good question.

Unfortunately the answer was not so straightforward.

Her mouth felt dry and, stalling for time, she shrugged. 'I don't know... It's so beautiful here, and I like running.'

Luis stared at her. His question had been in-nocuous enough, and yet she looked not just star-tled but dismayed.

'It *is* very beautiful,' he said slowly. 'And I'm glad you like running. But that doesn't answer my question. Why did you need to run?'

Cristina felt a familiar panic rising inside her. Her ribs seemed to be closing, so that it hurt to breathe. How was she supposed to answer him? One thing was certain: it wouldn't be with the truth. She could just picture his face changing, pity overshadowing his curiosity as quickly as a cloud blotting out the moon.

And yet his voice was gentle. 'I run too. Back in California. I have a house by the beach, and when I can't sleep I go for a run there.'

The painful sensation beneath her ribs was fad-ing.

'I run to escape.'

The words were out of her mouth before she'd even realised she'd spoken, and she felt a rush of fear. But, looking up at him, she saw that there was no pity in his eyes, no contempt curling his mouth.

'It doesn't have to be running. I just need to be moving. Otherwise I get these thoughts and I can't do anything.'

'What thoughts?'

'That I'm stupid. That I fail at everything.' Her

mouth twisted. 'That even though I run I'm always the runner-up.'

Luis felt his heart twist. Even without the sight of her hands clenching he could hear the strain in her voice, and he wanted more than anything to take away her pain. But he didn't know what to say. Bas had always been the one who knew the right words.

'You're not a runner-up,' he said gently. 'You got this job on merit. Justifiably. Because you're extraordinarily talented. You need to believe in yourself.'

Her mouth slanted upwards, but her smile was taut and unhappy. 'That's easy for you to say.'

Pressing the toe of her trainer into the unforgiving limestone, Cristina felt her body stiffen as he took a step towards her.

'No, it isn't.'

Something in his voice made her look up.

'Every day I miss my brother so much.' He glanced past her, his face clouded with emotion. 'That's why I come here. It was *our* place. It's where I feel closest to him,' he said simply. 'We used to sneak out at night. Even when he was really young Bas was a rule-breaker. He loved taking risks.'

Suddenly it hurt to look at his eyes, and she thought her cheeks might crack with the effort of keeping her expression even. 'And you don't?'

His gaze switched to her face. 'No. I tried...' He gave her a small, tight smile. 'After Bas died I thought that if I acted like him then maybe I could somehow keep him alive. So I started to take risks. I surfed the biggest waves I could find. I jumped out of planes—'

He made it sound ordinary, but she could feel the pain beneath his words.

'What happened?'

He shrugged. 'I had to stop. My parents...' His mouth thinned. 'They had enough to deal with as it was, and it was upsetting them.'

Around them, the air was heavy and silent. Even the waves seemed to have stilled.

'But you still ride motorbikes?'

He shook his head. 'That was a one-off. I was keeping a promise to my brother to take the road trip we always said we'd do.'

She nodded, but there was a choking feeling in her throat and she felt suddenly sick with herself.

Luis hadn't been playing at being a biker in Segovia. He'd been grieving for his brother.

Without thinking she reached out and took his hand. 'I'm sorry, Luis. About your brother. And about all those things I said—'

He shook his head. 'I deserved them. I was being self-righteous and unfair.'

His fingers tightened around hers, and she felt

her stomach squeeze. 'And I was stubborn and short-tempered,' she said.

'Sounds like we're made for each other,' he said softly, and she felt her heart clench as he leaned forward and kissed her.

Luis could hardly breathe. He hadn't intended to kiss her, but feeling her mouth soften against his made it impossible to still the longing in his blood. Deepening the kiss, he curled his arm around her waist and pulled her closer, his fingers threading through her hair. She tasted so sweet, and he wanted her so badly, and yet—

From somewhere deep inside he felt a ripple of panic rise to the surface, and slowly, dazedly, he kicked back against the relentless tide of his longing.

Gently, he broke the kiss and took a step backwards. 'I can't do this. I'm sorry.'

Her eyes widened and he swore silently, for the expression of shock and hurt on her face tore him up inside. But there was nothing he could do.

Cristina made him lose control, and he couldn't afford to lose control. She had the power to turn his life upside down and that wasn't something he could allow to happen—particularly now.

'Please forgive me...'

Her mouth quivered, and he knew that if she spoke, or touched him, he would change his mind.

He'd surrender to the desire beating in his blood whatever the consequences.

But she didn't say anything. Instead she backed away from him and then, turning, she ran lightly across the rocks.

He watched her head towards the pine trees, waiting until she'd disappeared before he breathed out.

It was the only choice, he told himself firmly. And the *right* choice. So why, then, he wondered as he started to walk slowly back towards the forest, did it feel as if he was making a mistake? And why did it hurt so damn much?

CHAPTER SEVEN

'To Sofia, my beautiful wife, *mi corazón*.' Lifting his glass of champagne, Agusto gazed at his wife, his dark grey eyes tender. *'Feliz cumpleaños.'*

Across the table, Cristina raised her glass and echoed his words.

'Happy Birthday, Mamá,' Luis said softly. 'Are you enjoying yourself?'

Sofia nodded, her eyes dropping to the beautiful sapphire necklace that had been her husband's birthday present to her. 'How could I not be, *cariño*?'

She ran her fingers lightly over the gleaming blue stones.

'This is one of my most favourite places in the world, and I've had the most wonderful day of being spoiled with all these beautiful gifts. But having you back, Lucho, is the best present of all. I'm so glad you could be here.'

Cristina felt her heart bump against her ribs. It was the first time she'd seen Luis properly since their encounter by the tidal pool the night before, so that was no doubt one reason why her nerves were humming. But it was also the first time she had heard Sofia call her son by that particular name, and the shock made swallowing the mouthful of champagne difficult.

For so long it had been easier to imagine that Lucho didn't exist except in her memory, but now her cheeks tingled as she realised that he was real. Real and sitting next to her.

Luis smiled. 'It's lovely to be here.'

Watching his face soften, Cristina held her breath. His smile was spectacular, but it was lucky that he didn't smile often, she thought. It was hard enough trying to keep control of herself under normal circumstances, but when he smiled—

She shivered, remembering the kiss they'd shared at the pool last night, and how simply and carelessly she had responded to the hard press of his body. How it had been Luis who had pulled away.

Her pulse quickened. Stumbling back over the rocks and through the pine trees, her self-control in shreds, she had tried telling herself that she'd had a lucky escape. That he shouldn't matter more to her than any man ever had or should.

Her fingers tightened around her glass.

In other words, too much.

He might have ended the kiss, but she had seen his face—seen that he was torn, barely controlling himself. He wanted her as badly as she wanted him, and suddenly, with an intensity that hurt, she wished that she could turn back time. Go back to that shabby little hotel room in Segovia when it had been just him and her and a bed, and no past or doubt or confusion.

Her heart gave a jump. Except that she still wouldn't trust herself not to try and make that chemistry between them into something more.

Her breathing stilled and, suddenly aware that the swell of conversation around her had stopped, she looked up and found three pairs of eyes watching her.

She blinked. 'Sorry—I was miles away.'

'It must have somewhere you were very happy.' Sofia smiled at her.

Glancing over at Luis, she found him watching her meditatively his dark gaze reaching inside of her. 'It was.' Meeting Sofia's gaze, she smiled. 'But I'm very happy to be here too.'

How could she not be?

La Almazara was not just a restaurant, it was a gastronomic legend. Despite its rural location on a tiny Balearic island, the converted olive mill attracted visitors from all over the world—she'd read somewhere that every year several hundred thousand people tried to reserve a table there but only a lucky few managed to get one.

Glancing down at her starter of bean soup and *jamón jabugo*, Cristina felt her pulse accelerate. It wasn't the exclusivity of the restaurant, or even the incredible food that made her feel like one of the lucky ones. It was the fact that Sofia, and Agusto had included her in their private family celebrations.

Her shoulders stiffened as she remembered back to the birthdays and Christmases after her father had left. Her mother had *tried*—they both had—but it had been such a struggle.

As an assistant housekeeper at one of the embassies in London, her mother worked long hours for a salary that had to support both of them and never quite did. On the plus side, her job was live-in, but the rooms had never felt like a home, and it had been difficult for either of them to relax there. And the nature of her mother's job meant that any private celebration always seemed secondary to the needs of the family in residence.

Oh, how she'd envied them—those people with their birthday cakes, their turkey and their tinsel, their board games. It had made her feel like the little match girl in that story, shivering outside in the cold, her nose pressed against the glass. And being a *paparazza* had only exacerbated her sense of being uninvited and unwelcome.

Only now here she was. A guest of the family.

She hadn't expected to be asked, and had initially declined. But Sofia had refused to accept her answer, and Agusto had backed her up, and in the end she'd capitulated.

Of course that hadn't stopped her worrying about what Luis would think when he found out. But ever since breakfast, when Sofia had invited her, she'd had other, more pressing concerns. Such as what the hell was she going to wear?

Glancing down at the green silk dress that skimmed her body and left her shoulders bare, she suddenly wanted to smile and keep on smiling. It hadn't taken long to answer that question. This trip was a work assignment, so she'd brought work clothes. Smartish trousers, shirts, a couple of skirts, some T-shirts, and—yes—one dress. Only it was navy, knee-length, and she'd only packed it because it didn't need ironing.

It certainly wasn't something she would have chosen to wear to an elegant restaurant like La Almazara, where presidents and painters mingled with Hollywood A-listers. She'd actually noticed an action movie star and his latest girlfriend on the way in.

It all felt slightly surreal—but not as surreal as returning to her room and finding this dress and a pair of beautiful gold ombré heels in her wardrobe, with a note from Sofia entreating her to wear them.

It was such a sweet gesture—and so generous. Even from just looking at the label inside the dress, and the red soles on the shoes, she had known that this outfit had cost more than her mother's monthly pay packet. And, although she had already thanked Sofia and Agusto, she wanted to make sure that they understood how grateful she was.

'It really was very good of you to invite me,' she said quickly. 'And so kind to give me this dress and the shoes. It was such a lovely idea.'

'*Querida!*' Leaning forward, Sofia smiled. 'You really don't need to keep thanking me. But, actually, it wasn't my idea.' Turning to her son, her face softened. 'It was Luis who suggested it this morning, when we were talking about the meal.'

Cristina froze, the other woman's words sending shock waves down her spine.

'Luis…?' She swallowed. 'But I thought—'

Sofia shook her head apologetically. 'I know you did, and I wanted to tell you the truth only Luis asked me not to—'

She broke off as a waiter approached the table with another bottle of champagne and spoke softly into her ear.

Turning towards her husband, she said, '*Cariño*, apparently Felipe and Isabella Alba are here to-night, and they have ordered this beautiful bottle of champagne for us.' She smiled at Cristina. 'Would you excuse us for a moment? We should go and thank them.'

Cristina nodded, and then, as they made their

way across the restaurant to an elderly couple, she turned towards Luis and said quietly, 'Why did you do that?'

His grey gaze rested on her face. 'This place has got a reputation for being swanky, and obviously you didn't know you were coming here…' He hesitated. 'I didn't want you to feel uncomfortable.'

His voice was gentle, but that wasn't why her skin grew warm. It was his words. There was nothing dramatic or striking about them. But they didn't need to be because they were true, and that was the most important thing. *She* had mattered to him, and he had cared about her enough to actually do something.

She steadied her breathing. 'Thank you for doing that for me. It was really thoughtful.'

He met her eyes and she felt her skin start to prickle. His smile might be spectacular, but that gaze… It seemed to pierce her skin, hold her still so that she couldn't move, couldn't look away, couldn't even breathe properly. No one had ever looked at her like that, with such intensity of focus, and her body tensed with fear and fascination.

'My pleasure.'

Caught off guard by her unaffected expression of gratitude, Luis felt his pulse skip a beat with guilt. It was true that he had been worried about her feeling uncomfortable, but that wasn't the only reason he'd talked to his mother. In so many ways Cristina reminded him of his brother. Like Bas, she was an odd mix of confident and vulnerable, and she was also stubborn and proud like him too. It had been all too easy to imagine her deciding that none of her clothes were suitable for going out in public with his parents and simply excusing herself.

And he'd wanted her to be there.

His jaw tightened. After he'd pushed her away last night he'd found it impossible to sleep. He'd just kept picturing the expression on her face— the hurt and confusion—and the way he'd let her leave. All night he'd been on the verge of going to her room so that he could explain. But of course that would have meant telling her why his brother was dead, so instead he had spoken to his mother.

'I'm glad you like it.' He gestured towards the dress. 'I was a little worried about the sizing, but...'

Her pulse skipped a beat. She gazed up at him, her eyes widening. '*You* chose it?'

The corner of his mouth slanted upwards. 'Well, my mother's been a valued customer of that designer for years, so they were happy to give me a little advice. But I had a kind of idea of what I wanted.'

He felt his groin harden. Not just *a kind of* idea.

It had been more like a full-blown Technicolor fantasy, and in that she'd actually been wearing very little. His breath caught in his throat as images of Cristina spilled again in his head—her long auburn hair tumbling in disarray over a crumpled pillow, her fingers tugging at buttons and zips—

Flattening down the ache of desire rising inside him, he cleared his throat. 'I wasn't sure about what colour to choose, and the general consensus seemed to be that black would be the safest option.'

Her face creased, but her honey-coloured gaze was steady on his as she said slowly, 'So you chose a green dress because…?'

He studied her face, seeing both curiosity, and vulnerability in her eyes. 'I suppose I don't think of you as the *safe* option,' he said softly. His eyes rested on her face and the air seemed to shimmer between them. 'Black is boring and sensible and unobtrusive, and the little black dress is a cliché. You're an original, *cariño*, and you deserve to be noticed.'

Cristina stared at him, his words tugging at the armour she had built around herself. For so long she had craved attention, but most of her life she had got it for the wrong reasons. And now Luis was telling her that she was an 'original'—not only that, she knew he meant it.

'Thank you.' Swallowing the emotion that was filling her chest, she lifted her chin. 'It's nice to know I'm not invisible to you any more.'

His eyes gleamed, the grey almost black beneath the restaurant's low-key lighting. 'You were never invisible to me, *cariño*.'

'You didn't notice me at the club. Or are you saying you walked into me on purpose?'

He smiled then—a long, slow, masculine smile that made her feel as though she'd drunk an entire bottle of champagne on her own.

'If you hadn't been wearing those shorts I might have been concentrating on where I was going.'

It was the first time he'd admitted what had really happened in the club, but it was more than just an admission of guilt. It was an olive branch.

Her heart began to thump jerkily against her ribs. 'So…are you concentrating now?'

His gaze flicked intently over her bare shoulders and down to the slight V of her cleavage and the curve of her waist.

'Of course I am.'

Watching his jaw tighten, she felt a jolt of heat punch her in the stomach.

'You're the most beautiful woman I've ever seen,' he said hoarsely.

Not as beautiful as you, she thought, her breath suddenly too light.

And she wasn't the only one to think so. Across

the restaurant, other female diners kept oh-so-casually glancing in his direction. But it wasn't only the women who were aware of him. When they'd followed the maître d' to their table there had been a sudden alertness among the men in the room, a recognition that they were in the presence of someone who commanded not just attention but respect. Why else would they all twist towards him like heliotropic flowers turning to face the sun?

She could feel herself doing it too, feel her body pulling towards him, beyond any kind of conscious control.

Their eyes met.

'You look—' she began, and then she frowned. 'You're not wearing a shirt and tie.'

Glancing down at his black polo shirt, he shrugged. 'I felt like a change.'

This sudden switch from smart to casual was disorientating—or it would have been had Luis not chosen that moment to take her hand under the table. As she felt his fingers weave through hers it suddenly didn't seem to matter what he was wearing.

Dry-mouthed, she stared at him mutely as Sofia and Agusto sat back down—

'Excuse me, *señorita*. Would you like sparkling or still water?'

Startled, she looked up at the waiter and smiled

mechanically. 'Still, please. Just a drop,' she added as he also went to fill up her champagne glass. 'Are you not drinking?' she asked Luis. She'd noticed that he was once again sticking to soft drinks.

He shrugged. 'I've got a couple of conference calls tomorrow, so I need to keep a clear head.'

She nodded, intrigued. Surely his mother's six-tieth birthday was a special enough occasion to have a glass of champagne?

His mother smiled. 'Champagne used to give me such a headache when I was younger. Do you remember, Agusto, those cocktails your parents used to love so much?'

Taking his wife's hand, Agusto laughed. 'Not really, *cariño*, but I think that was the point.' Turning to Cristina he said, 'They used to mix champagne with sherry. It was absolutely lethal.' His eyes gleamed. 'Wouldn't you agree, Luis?'

Beside her, Luis groaned. 'I was young and naive—'

'What happened?'

She twisted towards him. Her pulse was dancing, and she knew that her pleasure at hearing about his life was all over her face, but just for once she didn't feel the need to hide her emotions.

He shook his head. 'I must have been about sixteen. My grandparents were having a party, and all the little old ladies were drinking cocktails, one after another. Bas and I thought they must be harmless, so we had one, and then two, three—' He grimaced. 'Harmless! I don't think I've ever felt so ill!'

'Were you sick?'

Shuddering, he shook his head. 'No. But neither of us could stand up, let alone speak. In the end we had to go to bed.'

His father laughed. 'What my son is failing to mention is that they went to bed at half past eight, and the bed in question belonged to my parents' elderly mastiffs.'

Cristina burst out laughing. 'I can't believe you slept in a dogs' bed.'

'It was only the once.' Sofia smiled at her son affectionately. 'Luis has always been cautious. Even when he was a little boy he liked to do things properly, to do the right thing. And nothing's changed—has it, Agusto?'

There was a short, strained silence, and Cristina could almost feel the atmosphere around the table shift.

'He's a very good son,' Agusto said stiffly. 'But I'm not sure if deliberately living on the other side of the world from your family can ever really be described as doing "the right thing"—'

'Agusto…' Sofia said softly, but Luis interrupted her.

'It's fine, Mamá.' He met his father's gaze. 'Papá,

I know you're upset with me, and I totally understand why you feel the way you do. But you have to understand and accept that my life is in California now.'

He spoke quietly, but with calm determination, and Cristina knew that this was not the first time he'd had this conversation with his father. Nor, judging by the glint in Agusto's eyes, would it be the last.

Her hunch was quickly confirmed as the older man said stubbornly, 'But that's just it. I don't understand. This is your home, Luis. Your life should be *here*. You have a family who loves you and needs you.' He frowned. 'And a legacy that has—'

Cristina felt her pulse jump as abruptly Luis pulled his hand free of hers.

'Ah, *now* we're getting to the truth.'

Luis drew a breath. He was deliberately stoking his anger, but beneath it he could already feel the old familiar guilt rising inside him.

Desperately he tried to hang on to his fury. 'It's not actually about family at all and it never has been. It's about the business.'

'They're one and the same.'

Despite having heard them since he was old enough to understand, his father's words still had the power to catch him off guard—but it was the sadness in Agusto's voice that made him grip the edges of the table.

Wincing inwardly, he shook his head. 'Not to me.'

Watching his father's shoulders slump, he felt a dull ache spread through his chest.

'I'm an old man, Luis. I can't run the business for ever.'

Hating himself, he reached over and gripped Agusto's arm. 'I know. But, Papá, we've been over this a hundred times, and each time I've given you my answer—'

His father shook his head. 'No. What you've given me is an excuse, Luis, and I don't understand why you feel that way. But I will accept it.' Lifting his hand, he patted his son's hand. 'And your mother's right. You are a good son, and we both love you very much. We're proud of what you've achieved.'

'I know. And I love coming to visit.' Frowning, he turned to his mother. 'Sorry, Mamá.'

'I'm sorry too, *cariño*.'

Sofia seemed more resigned than anything else, Cristina thought. No doubt she was used to it— and, given how close Luis and his father were, it probably sounded worse that it had seemed to her.

Clearly that was true, for moments later they were all chatting easily about Luis's ranch. But, despite the fact that conversation flowed smoothly for the rest of the evening, she couldn't shift the feeling that Luis had been lying to his parents.

Worse, she was pretty sure he'd been lying to himself too.

When they returned to the island Sofia and Agusto excused themselves, and Cristina found herself alone with Luis.

Given what had happened the previous night, she had supposed he would follow his parents and turn in, so she was surprised when he turned to her and said, 'I'm going to have a drink—would you care to join me?'

'Oh.' She gazed at him uncertainly. 'Well, that—'

She broke off as he raised his hands placatingly.

'I just meant coffee or tea.'

'So no champagne cocktail, then?' The urge to tease overwhelmed any caution she might have had about being alone with him.

His eyes gleamed, and she felt a tiny flicker of excitement as the corners of his mouth tugged upwards.

'Sadly we don't have any dogs, and the floors look awfully hard and cold.'

'Tea would be lovely, then.'

It was the first time she'd been in the kitchen. Although it was large, it felt surprisingly homely. 'This is lovely.'

He glanced over at her. 'We seem to have every flavour of tea imaginable, so—'

'Actually, builders' would be fine.'

'Builders'?' He raised an eyebrow.

She laughed. 'It's what English people call breakfast tea. I like it strong with lots of milk. Thank you.'

After Luis had made the tea, they sat on opposite sides of the breakfast bar. She had thought she would have to do the talking, but it was Luis who spoke first.

'Did you enjoy the meal?'

'Yes, it was incredible. I've never eaten food like that.' Remembering the tension between him and Agusto, she hesitated. Then, 'Do you think your mother enjoyed herself?'

There was a tiny pause. Luis stared at her. 'Of course. It's her favourite restaurant.'

She waited for a moment, and when he didn't say anything else, just stared pointedly past her, she felt her cheeks start to tingle. She could just back off, talk about the food, or maybe the design of this kitchen, but she was still struggling to make sense of what had happened over dinner.

Luis was fiercely protective of his parents, and yet even though his father had as good as asked him to stay he'd refused. In fact he'd shut the entire conversation down even though she knew it had hurt him to do so. She didn't know how she knew—she just knew that it had. And that it had hurt her to feel his pain.

She bit her lip. Her heart started to race. 'She loves having you here.'

'I love being here.'

There was a definite warning tone in the coolness of his voice, but for some totally illogical reason that only made her more determined to talk to him about what had happened.

'But what about when you go back to California?'

He looked over at her, his grey eyes suddenly cool and hostile, as though she was some kind of intruder.

'I'm not sure why you think that's any of your business, but even if it were I don't want to talk about it.'

The expression on his face made her skin freeze to her bones. It was as though they were back on that balcony and he was that same man who had accused her of being a cold-hearted, self-serving parasite. But wasn't that what *she* always did when she was upset and scared? Lashed out at people, pushed them away...

Striving to stay calm, she said, 'I know. And I get that. But what I don't get is why you don't want to talk to your father about it.' Her breath was weaving in and out of her lungs too fast, as though she'd been running. 'I'm not judging you—it's just that I don't have that kind of relationship with my father, and—'

And I'd kill even to hear his voice, much less have him tell me he loves me and needs me.

She finished the sentence in her head, her stomach churning with panic at the thought of having revealed the truth, even obliquely. The truth that she hadn't mattered to the one man whose love and protection should have been unconditional.

Luis felt his muscles tighten. He felt ashamed of the way he'd acted at dinner. Yes, maybe his father shouldn't have brought it up, but he'd handled it badly. Or rather he hadn't handled it at all. Instead he'd done what he always did when his parents discussed the bank, or him returning to Segovia, he'd got irritated and defensive. And tonight he'd let it get completely out of hand.

It was unforgivable. He shouldn't have done it—and wouldn't have except that he hadn't been thinking straight.

And it was her fault. He glanced over to where Cristina sat watching him, and suddenly it was easier to blame her than himself.

'You don't need to "get" it. You're not here to practise your amateur psychology. You're here to photograph my parents. *Allegedly*, anyway.'

'What does that mean?' Her eyes were suddenly narrow and blazing with anger.

'It means that just because I bought you a dress

it doesn't mean that I've bought that whole little-girl-lost-on-the-streets-of-Segovia act. Do you really think I believe in that kind of coincidence?'

She stood up so fast that the stool she'd been sitting on spun away from her.

'*What* kind of coincidence?' She was practically shouting now.

'Oh, you know, Cristina—the sort where we end up in bed one night and then the next day it turns out that you just happen to be taking my parents' photographs.'

The blood drained from her face. 'It wasn't like that and you know it.' She took a step backwards, her body trembling with anger. 'And you know something else too. You might not believe in coincidences but I don't believe in *you*. I think everything that comes of your mouth is a lie. Not just about me. But about yourself. About who you are, and what you want.'

Her hands curling into fists, she picked up the stool and slammed it back under the counter.

'And, whatever you might think of me, your parents don't deserve that. What's more, you don't deserve *them*!'

The room fell silent.

Cristina breathed out shakily. She wanted to say more, but one look at his still, set face told her there was no point. And, really, why should she waste any more time on him? It might not have sounded like much to him but she had laid her soul bare and—

'You're right.'

She glanced up at him and felt her stomach lurch. His skin was no longer taut but shifting, like ice cracking on a frozen lake, as pain rippled across his face.

'I *am* lying,' he mumbled. 'I don't think you're that person and I shouldn't have said I did. You didn't deserve it.' He looked past her, his eyes dark with shame and unease.

But it was his voice as much as his words that startled her. The strain she could hear in it was heartbreaking.

'And they don't deserve a son like me.'

He stopped short, as though it hurt too much for him to go on, and looking across at his stricken face, Cristina felt her anger start to evaporate.

'Look, I shouldn't have said that. It's nothing to do with me. Your father will find someone else to run the bank—'

His face twisted. 'You don't understand. It's not just the bank.'

She stared at him, her body stiffening as though she was bracing herself for a blow. 'What do you mean?'

His face tightened, the skin taut across his cheekbones. 'I did something unforgivable.'

Shaken, she shook her head automatically. 'I

doubt that. Whatever it was your parents would
forgive you. They *would*,' she repeated as he
shook his head.

'No, they wouldn't. They couldn't. You see, it
was my fault. Don't you understand? None of it
would have happened if—'

Only she didn't see. Or understand any of what
he was saying. But she knew instinctively that it
was what he wasn't saying that was really important.

'If what?'

He ran his hand tiredly over his face. 'It doesn't
matter—'

Reaching out, she grabbed his arm. 'It does
to me.'

Looking into her eyes, Luis felt his breathing
trip in his throat. She was telling the truth. It did
matter to her. But still he couldn't speak.

As though sensing his silence was beyond his
control, she said quietly, 'If you're not happy in
California why do you stay there?'

He looked up at her slowly. 'I never said I
wasn't happy there.'

'But you did.' Her fingers tightened on his arm.
'You said you don't sleep. That you have to run.'
She hesitated. 'What is it, Luis? What are you
running from?'

The directness of her question caught him off-
guard. And, looking up into her eyes, he suddenly

wanted to answer her—for he could see that she was worried.

About him.

And that she cared.

About him.

But… 'I don't know when to start,' he said slowly.

Or maybe he meant *how* to start, for he'd spent so long trying not to think about that night that he didn't seem to have the words to tell his story.

Thinking about her own pain, Cristina felt a knot in her stomach. 'Usually it's not *when* that matters—it's who.' She glanced around the kitchen. 'And sometimes where. Let's get some air.'

It wasn't a question, but after a moment he nodded.

Away from the house Luis immediately felt calmer, and as they walked down to the beach it suddenly seemed the most natural thing in the world to start talking about his brother.

'Bas and I went to this party up in the hills. I didn't really want to go. I'd just finished my master's, and all I wanted to do was sleep. But he wouldn't hear of it and my mother thought I needed to relax.'

They had reached the beach, and as he stopped and stared at the sea Cristina felt a sudden panic that he'd changed his mind. That he was going to clam up, lock himself away.

Clearing her throat, she said quietly, 'Did you have fun?'

He shrugged. 'Not really. I liked my brother's friends but I was four years younger than them. We didn't really have a lot in common, and I felt a bit left out. I drank a bit too much—' The corner of his mouth dipped. 'And I was tired, a bit fed up, so I was just about to leave when…' He paused, his jaw tightening. 'When I saw her. She was already watching me.'

Glancing down, Luis pushed the toe of his shoe into the sand, wishing it was as easy to push away the past.

'Afterwards I couldn't believe how naive I'd been.'

Even now he could still remember the shock, the disbelief, and then the breathtaking shame of his vanity and stupidity.

Sick with misery, he turned, but Cristina stepped in front of him.

'After what?'

The guilt and despair on his face almost split her in two.

'After I found out she was *paparazzi*. Only by then it was too late. I'd already slept with her,' he said woodenly. 'And told her that my brother had hooked up with a Hollywood actress who was in town, making a film. She told her grubby little mates and that's how he died—crashing his car, trying to escape a bunch of photographers.'

His face was stiff with misery and pain.

'I was the last person to speak to him. He called and told me to have fun, and he said—' he was suddenly struggling to speak '—and he said that he loved me.'

Cristina couldn't speak. Her mouth wouldn't open and there was a hard lump in her throat that seemed to be stopping the words from coming out. But she couldn't just say *nothing*.

'I'm so sorry, Luis.'

Her words sounded trite, but Luis didn't even seem to hear them.

'If I'd been more careful—'

'But you didn't know—'

'No, because I was too drunk and too busy thinking what a man I was.'

'You're not like that.'

Her hands clenched together as she remembered him drinking water at his mother's birthday dinner. It wasn't just champagne or wine he didn't drink. It was all alcohol.

'You can't blame yourself.'

He looked at her then, his eyes unfocused and dull with pain. 'But I *am* to blame. And that's why I have to live in California. I can't live in Spain and not take over the bank. That was *Bas's* birthright and I took it away from him. I took him away from my parents and I don't deserve their love.'

'Yes, you do.' She took a step closer. 'You made a mistake, and nobody gets through life without making mistakes. What happened to Bas was a terrible, tragic accident, but you can't keep punishing yourself for being young and naive.'

She hesitated.

'Sometimes it's easier to judge yourself harshly than to look at the bigger picture. But turning in on yourself doesn't solve anything. It just damages everyone around you.' Her heart contracted as she pictured her mother's anxious face. 'And if they're around you it's because they care.'

Luis stared at her in silence. After their initial shock at his story most people would surely be wrapped up in their own dismay or disgust. But Cristina seemed to care about him and his feelings—not hers.

'None of us can change the past. It won't matter how unhappy you make yourself, or how much you think you deserve to feel unhappy, you can't bring your brother back.'

Reaching out, she took his hand.

'You taking over the bank would not be disrespectful to your brother's memory. It would just be you taking care of your parents. Being their son—the son you were before Bas died, and the son you will always be.'

She knew she was right, but she'd been wrong about almost everything else. Luis was nothing like her father—a man who had never taken responsibility for his actions, let alone acknowledged them. He had not only accepted the blame for Bas's death he had punished himself for it, even going so far as to exile himself from his homeland and his parents.

She felt his fingers tighten around hers.

'I miss him so much…'

'I know. But forgiving yourself doesn't mean forgetting Bas. Your parents love you, Luis, and they need you. So you need to forgive yourself and come back home.'

Luis nodded, and then, leaning forward, he cupped her chin in his hand and tilted her face upwards. 'Were you always this smart?'

She smiled. 'Of course. Hadn't you noticed?'

Yesterday he had pushed her away, but now, with her warm body so close to his, it was hard to remember exactly why he'd felt he should do that. Her eyes were soft and light and, feeling his heart start to beat faster, he shook his head.

'I guess I was distracted.'

'By what?'

Her voice was shaking slightly, and he could see the pulse twitching at the base of his throat.

'By this,' he whispered and, lowering his mouth to hers, he kissed her.

Behind them the waves splashed against the sand, as he slowly wrapped his arms around her and deepened the kiss. Still kissing, they stripped each other naked, and then they slid down onto their discarded clothes.

His fingers were slipping over her bare skin, their touch light and yet electric, and his mouth was warm and hungry against her lips. His body felt hollow with desire as she pulled him closer, curling her hand around the curve of his neck, their clothes twisting beneath them as she turned her face into the hard muscles of his chest.

She felt his hand between her trembling thighs, his fingers gently parting her legs, their touch setting her adrift from her body.

'Look at me,' he whispered. 'I want to see your eyes.'

Breath quickening, she looked up at him, and he cupped her buttocks and thrust into her. And then his body was stretching hers and she was pushing back, tugging him deeper, until heat flowered inside her and she arched upwards as his shuddering body surged forward again and again, like the waves that were breaking against the beach...

CHAPTER EIGHT

LUIS WOKE TO the sound of his alarm. Eyes closed, he fumbled across the bed, his fingers reaching for his phone on his bedside cabinet. Only his phone wasn't there.

'What the hell…?' he muttered, rolling onto his side.

But of course he wasn't in his bedroom, and now he was actually awake he realised that it wasn't his alarm either.

'Sorry, sorry—did it wake you?'

Emerging from the bathroom, a towel clutched in front of her throat, another wrapped turban-style around her head, Cristina rummaged in the small clutch bag she had taken to the restaurant and pulled out her phone.

Holding it up, she swiped the screen. 'I meant to turn it off last night, but I…'

'You what?' Luis said softly.

His eyes dropped to the towel and he felt his fingers twitch as he wondered how she had managed to arrange it so that it seemed to both hide everything and yet hint at the spectacular body that lay beneath.

Her face stilled. 'I got distracted.'

'Oh, is that what happened?'

His muscles tensed, and a pulse began to beat beneath his skin as she walked towards him. He was still struggling to come to terms with what had happened last night—not just the fact that they'd ended up naked and making love on the beach, but that he'd told her about Bas, and about his part in his brother's death.

He hadn't planned to tell her. Hell, he hadn't planned on telling *anyone*, ever—let alone a woman who barely knew him. But Cristina had surprised him by actually listening to what he'd said. More surprisingly, her words hadn't simply been catch-all platitudes. He had felt as if she knew him—almost as if she'd known him for a long time.

'I don't know. Is it?'

Her light brown eyes were watching his, and it was suddenly difficult to manage his breathing, let alone his thoughts. And, to be fair, it wasn't a question he'd ever been asked before?

But then he'd never done this before. He'd had a couple of one-night stands, both of which had been short and satisfactory but neither of which had required post-coital conversation. And in his other, more serious relationships sex had happened after the ground rules about intimacy and commitment had been established.

That first time in Segovia it had been simple. Just raw, powerful sexual need, no speaking required. It had been about bodies, and skin, and sweat, and one sole aim—his need to take her. He had practically torn her clothes off her, such had been the frenzy of his desire.

But last night—this morning—had been more than just sex.

His throat tightened. He could just be honest and tell her that. Tell her that it had felt good, incredible. And not just the sex but holding her against him and feeling her arm curled over his chest. He could tell her that part had felt better than good. That it had turned him inside out, and that no woman had ever made him feel like that.

Only he wouldn't tell her any of that—not without knowing what she was thinking.

'It was sensational, whatever it was,' she said.

He nodded, heat sweeping through him as she unwound the towel from around her head and began rubbing it slowly over her hair in a way that made his fingers itch to unwind the one around her body.

'So what happens next?'

The words were out of his mouth before he'd even known he was going to say them, and it was too late to take them back. Too late to do anything but meet her gaze.

Glancing over at his lean, naked body, Cristina felt heat pool low in her pelvis. Waking beside him in the darkness, his legs entwined with hers, she had thought she was dreaming, and it had taken several moments before her stunned brain could accept that Luis was there in her bed. Heart pounding, she had watched him sleep, mesmerised by his beauty, wishing silently that it could last for ever. That it could be just the two of them together and one endless night.

Listening to Luis talk about his brother, knowing that his loyalty and love for his family were absolute, she'd felt a fierce protective urge towards him, and more than anything she had wanted to take away his pain. But then at some point he had taken away her pain too.

She had never felt so completely desired. Or so needed.

It should have felt wonderful, and it had—it did—only…

Her breath felt suddenly leaden in her chest. Only facts were facts, and nothing could last for ever. Sooner or later Luis would discover that not only was she a mass of insecurities but she also had a humiliating past. And then that would be that.

She felt a ripple of fear snake across her skin. What if no man ever made her feel like that again?

Her pulse trembled.

That was, of course, a rhetorical question, for

how could she ever recreate the last few days? All this—the island, the *fortaleza*, Luis—it wasn't real life. Or not her real life anyway. Soon she would be back in London and then her time with Luis would be nothing more than a beautiful memory.

But they were both adults, both single, and the sexual spark between them was powerful enough to light up the entire Iberian peninsula.

So why not make the most of it?

Looking down at his gorgeous body, she swallowed hard. 'I don't know, but I do know that I like you. And I think you like me.'

Luis felt his breath catch a little. The simplicity of her words as much as the proximity of her warm, near-naked body was making his pulse jump in his chest, and it took a moment to steady both his breathing and his expression.

Right now, being with Cristina felt like a no-brainer. No one had come close to making him feel like she did, but—

'You're not looking for something serious?'

She shook her head. 'I'm not.'

'My parents—'

'Don't need to know,' she said quickly. 'This is just between us.'

And if he'd been close to losing control before he almost lost it there and then as casually she undid the towel and let it drop from her body.

'Just you and me,' she said huskily.

Kneeling on the bed, she straddled him, her naked body pressing against his erection. Instinctively his hands slid up around her waist, then higher to her breasts, and he gazed up at her, his breath stilling in his throat as he felt her shiver.

Slowly he stroked her nipples, his heart kicking against his ribs as he felt the tips swell and harden beneath his fingers. Watching her soft brown eyes dilate, he lifted his head and kissed her.

'You're so beautiful,' he whispered against her mouth.

Breathing shallowly, Cristina reached down to steady herself, and at the touch of her hands he broke away from her mouth, his head falling back against the pillow, the breath hissing between his teeth.

His eyes were fixed on her face, intent and impossibly dark, their grey swallowed up by the black of his pupils. Muscles clenching, she rolled back and forth on his body in time to the pulse beating between her thighs.

'Luis…' she murmured and, bending her head, she kissed him, brushing her lips over his, her fingers stroking his arms, his chest, down over the furrows of muscle on his stomach, then closing over the length of his erection.

He jerked against her and, maddened by her

touch, he caught her fingers, tightening his hand around hers as she fed him into herself.

'Ah, Cristina…' He groaned, his pulse accelerating. She was so tight and warm and wet, and suddenly he knew he could wait no longer.

Rocking against him, Cristina felt the change, felt his body growing harder and tauter even as the ball of heat rolling inside her moved faster and faster. And then, just as she knew she could take no more, he grabbed both her hands and, pressing them into the mattress, thrust upwards as she arched into him.

Later—much later—she lay and watched him as he collected his clothes from the floor, where she'd stripped them off him earlier that morning. They had made love again, then taken a shower together, and ended up making love until the water had run cold, and they had stumbled, laughing, back into the bedroom and into bed.

Even just thinking about him moving against her made her skin prickle, for she knew how it felt to have him deep inside her, to have his mouth and hands roam at will over her body.

Her eyes rested on his hands—those same hands that had given her such pleasure—and she felt a pang like hunger.

And then, just like that, her brain jumped forward and she frowned. 'We missed breakfast.'

Luis glanced over at her from where he was

buckling his belt. 'I'm sure Pilar will be happy to make you anything you wish, *cariño.*'

She shook her head. 'I'm not hungry—well, I *am*, a little—but what about your parents? Won't they wonder where you are? Where *I* am.'

'No and maybe. I quite often don't eat breakfast with them when I'm here, and they probably think you're having a lie-in.'

She relaxed slightly, and then felt her heart give a jolt as he picked up his shirt.

'But you're wearing the same clothes as yesterday. They're going to notice that, and then—'

Crossing the room, Luis sat down on the bed beside her. 'Then what?'

Reaching forward, he pulled her onto his lap, his dark eyes resting on her face, his bare muscular chest brushing her breasts.

'I'm thirty, *cariño*, not thirteen.' He held her gaze. 'I thought you were okay about all this?'

'I am,' she said quickly. 'I just don't want them to get the wrong idea.'

He smiled then—a slow smile that made her body surge back to life—and she wanted him again, so badly that she could hardly remember what they were talking about.

'No, you don't want them to get the *right* idea.'

He gazed down at her, eyes narrowing, and she felt her breath catch as his fingers began caressing her hipbone. Quickly, before her greedy body could override her brain, she wriggled out of his grip and stood up.

'Luis, stop… I need to get some clothes on and go and do some work, and so do you.'

She dressed quickly, expecting him to do the same, but when she returned from cleaning her teeth he was still sitting there, his shirt dangling from his fingers.

Her heart seemed suddenly to be beating too fast. 'What is it? What's wrong?'

He was silent a moment, and then he said quietly, 'I've decided to talk to my parents.'

She heard the tension in his voice before she registered the implication of his words. 'You mean about Bas?'

He nodded. 'I need to tell them what happened. What I did.'

Reaching out, she pressed her hand against his cheek and stroked it gently with her thumb. 'I know you do. And this is the right time.'

'Is it?' He looked up at her, his grey eyes searching hers.

'Yes.' She nodded. 'Get dressed, and I'll come with you.

Cristina watched Luis walk away, and then, turning, she walked quickly outside, towards the terraced gardens. Her heart was bumping against her ribs—but not because she was worried about what Agusto and Sofia would say.

Blinded by guilt and grief, Luis had been unable to see the obvious. But she knew that his parents loved him unconditionally and would forgive him anything.

Why, then, did she feel so hollowed out? So empty. So alone.

The heat of the flagstones was burning through the thin soles of her sandals and, ducking into the marble folly at the end of the path, she breathed out with relief. It was cool and still inside, but while she might have escaped the sun there was no escape from the turmoil of her thoughts.

Gazing out across the smooth blue Mediterranean, she felt her throat tighten.

Other men had wanted her. But just for a moment Luis had needed her. She had been in his life for more than just sex.

Only now that moment had passed and she would go back to being an outsider.

Remembering the day when she'd finally realised that that was what she was, and would always be to her father, she shivered. His rejection had been total. Worse, it had been public too.

But so what if it had? Her mother loved her and that should be enough.

Except that it wasn't.

And there didn't seem to be anything she could do about it.

The blood was singing in her ears.

Or was there?

Reaching into her pocket, she pulled out her phone and scrolled down the list of calls on the screen. It was the same number. Laura's number.

A girl—a woman now—whose voice had up-ended her life.

Her half-sister.

They had never met—you couldn't call scream-ing abuse in front of someone a meeting. But Cris-tina knew who Laura was.

She'd stalked her on social media—knew that they were the same age and that Laura's birthday was exactly three months after hers, that they looked alike. Or they would if Laura dyed her hair red and swapped her preppy chinos and loafers for frayed denim and sky-high stilettos.

But that didn't seem very likely. Unlike her, Laura had been a high achiever at school, studied History of Art at Bryn Mawr College and now had a job at the Metropolitan Museum of Art.

Cristina's hands were trembling.

Laura was everything she'd wanted to be and everything her father had wanted from a daugh-ter. There was nothing to be gained from talk-ing to her.

Maybe. But there was infinitely more to be lost

by burying her head in the sand. For hadn't she encouraged Luis to face his worst fears? If she was too scared to speak to her super-successful and cool half-sister then she was not only a coward, but a hypocrite.

She lifted her chin and pressed Laura's number. It rang twice, then—'Hello? Cristina?'

Her pulse soared. For a moment she almost hung up, and then, biting back the panic filling her mouth, she said, 'You wanted to talk to me.'

'Yes.'

There was a short, stunned silence, and she could almost picture the expression of shock and disbelief on Laura's face.

'Yes, I do. I just can't believe you called me back.'

There was a noticeable shake in her voice, and it occurred to Cristina that Laura sounded more nervous than she did. Even though that made her feel marginally better, it still took courage for her to ask the question that had been bothering her ever since her half-sister had started calling her.

'How did you get my number?'

She heard Laura clear her throat.

'It wasn't that hard. I found you on social media, and you were tagged in a photo with some other *paparazzi*. So I rang round all the agencies and someone told me you were working for Grace.'

Cristina flinched inwardly. She felt suddenly

horribly exposed—almost as though she'd been caught on camera herself. 'You know Grace?'

'No, but obviously I've heard of her, so I rang the magazine.' She paused. 'I didn't say anything about us, I just said that I wanted to talk to you about that photo you took of Bornstein. We're doing an exhibition of his sculptures next year...' Her voice trailed off.

Feeling calmer, Cristina said slowly, 'So why do you want to talk to me?'

'I'm sorry... I don't know really know how to tell you this so I'm just going to say it. Papá is in hospital.'

Christina said nothing. Still clutching her phone, she stared blankly at the sea, a choked feeling in her throat. Having more or less stopped talking about her father, it was a shock to hear Laura referring to him so naturally. But more shocking still was the news that he was ill.

Only really why should she care? When had Enrique Lastra last cared about *her*—if ever? She'd had her appendix out when she was nineteen, where had he been then?

'Well, thank you for telling me,' she said woodenly. 'But I don't really see what that's got to do with me.'

There was a silence, then Laura said quietly, 'I thought you'd want to know. He's your father too, Cristina.'

'Not for a long time he hasn't been. Actually, make that never.' She hated hearing the bitterness in her voice but it was impossible to stop it.

'I know how you must feel—'

'I doubt that. In fact I'm pretty damn sure you *don't*.'

She knew she was being unfair. Laura was not responsible for their father's actions any more than she was, but she couldn't help herself.

'You're right. I don't, and it was a stupid thing to say. But I really think you should see him.'

'I'm not going to fly to America to see a man who's barely—'

'He's not in America, Cristina. He's in Spain. Just like you. In Madrid. And he's dying.'

Dying!

Her heart felt like a lump of ice. The breath in her throat had turned to lead.

'He can't be...' she whispered.

'I'm sorry. But he is.'

Cristina could hear the ache in Laura's voice.

'That isn't why I've been ringing you, though.' She hesitated. 'He wants to see you.'

Cristina covered her mouth with her hand. She had waited so long to hear those words. Played out so many scenarios inside her head. But now that it had happened she didn't know what to say.

'I don't know,' she said finally. 'I need to think about it.'

'But there's not much time—'

She cut through Laura's pleading words. 'I can't talk about this now. I'm working and—'

'Surely they'd understand?'

From somewhere outside she could hear the sound of footsteps and she stood up hurriedly.

'Look, Laura, I'm not like you. I need this job.' She thought of her mother, and the fold-out bed she used every time she visited her. 'I need the money. So please don't call me again. I'll ring you when I can.'

She hung up, and turned just as Luis stepped into the folly.

For a moment he just stared at her, his eyes dark and intent, his shoulders blocking the entrance. 'So,' he remarked in a voice that made a chill slip over her skin, 'who was that on the phone?'

He'd been looking for her for at least half an hour.

It had been a gruelling but ultimately rewarding morning. Telling his parents had been easier and less painful than he'd imagined it would be.

Easier because he'd already confided in Cristina, and less painful because both Agusto and Sofia were so distressed by the fact that he had not only felt responsible for Bas's death but coped with his guilt alone.

'Of *course* it wasn't your fault, Luis.' Agusto had shaken his head. 'Whatever you told that reporter, Baltasar was a grown man. He could have simply stopped the car. Or let the *paparazzi* follow him. Your brother's death was a terrible accident, and your mother and I agreed on that a long time ago.'

He'd felt calmer then, and lighter, as though something had been eased from his shoulders. And it was all thanks to Cristina. If she hadn't been there—

His heart had contracted and he had known he needed to find her and thank her.

Only she hadn't been in the house, and Pilar hadn't seen her either. He'd tried calling her, but her phone had been engaged. It was only by chance that he'd caught sight of her as he was striding past the folly.

But as she'd turned to face him his anticipation of talking to her had given way to a mix of doubt and disquiet, for even if he hadn't heard the urgency and panic in her voice, her cheeks were flushed with guilt.

'Who were you talking to?' He spoke calmly, but watching her trying to compose that beautiful face—that beautiful, disingenuous face—into a mask of innocence, he felt as though a hurricane was raging through his body. He remembered all the times her phone had rung and she'd ignored it.

She gave him an awkward shrug. 'Oh, it was just Grace. I sent over some of the shots.'

'What did she think?'

It was difficult to say what was more impressive, he thought savagely. Her ability to lie so efficaciously or the detachment in his own voice.

The flags of colour on her cheekbones grew darker as she smiled. 'She hasn't looked at them yet.'

Cristina thought her lips might crack with the effort of smiling. It felt wrong, lying to Luis, but what was she supposed to tell him? The truth?

Her stomach lurched. No, anything was better than that. Particularly as his mood seemed to have shifted.

Glancing at his face, she let her brain loop back to earlier that morning, and her heart thumped as she realised why he was acting so oddly.

'So how did it go with your parents? Was it okay?'

He held her gaze. 'Is that what this is about? My family secrets? If so, I hope they're paying you well, because by the time you step off this island I'll have made certain you never work again.'

The stone floor seemed to ripple beneath her feet and she took a step backwards. 'What are you talking about? I don't understand—'

'Then let me enlighten you.'

He stepped forward and, taking the phone from her hand, swiped the screen. Then, eyes narrowing, he thrust it in front of her face.

'According to your contacts list you were talking to Laura, *not* Grace, and that makes you a liar.'

Watching the shock and then resignation on her face, Luis thought he might throw up. He had believed her. Not just believed her but confided in her.

'It— It's not what you think,' she stammered.

'No,' he said coldly. 'It probably never is with you, Cristina.' His mouth curled with contempt. 'Now, I could make some accusations and you could deny them—but, frankly, I don't want to waste that much time on you. So I think I'll just call this Laura and find out which grubby little rag she's working for—'

'No. You can't call her!' Cristina lunged for the phone but he held it out of her reach.

'But I can.'

His eyes were blazing with anger, and to her horror she realised that he was serious.

'Please—she's not a reporter. She works at a museum.'

He glanced over at her but didn't lower his arm. 'And she's ringing you because…?'

She stared at him dumbly, pain swelling in her chest. 'She's my half-sister.'

Luis stared at her. No one except maybe a professional actress could fake the shock and pain in her eyes. She was telling the truth, but…

'But why didn't you answer her calls?' He glanced down at the screen. 'She must have rung you a hundred times.'

She was looking at him, but he could tell that she wasn't really seeing him, maybe not even hearing him. Incredibly her shock and distress outweighed his own.

He lowered his arm. 'I didn't know you had a sister—half-sister, I mean. You haven't mentioned her. Are you not close?'

Cristina shook her head. 'Actually, I've never met her.'

Looking up at him, she saw the confusion in his eyes and quickly looked away. What had possessed her to tell him the truth? It had been stupid—but she wasn't thinking straight.

'So why does she keep ringing you?'

Her heart began to thump, but there was nothing left now but the truth.

'She's been trying to get in touch with me because…well, because my father's in hospital. In Madrid.' She took a breath. 'He's dying.'

'Dying—?'

He sounded not just confused now, but stunned.

'Why didn't you tell me?' His eyes were wide with shock and remorse. 'Look, take the helicopter—please. Tomas will fly you wherever you need to go—'

'No, thank you,' she said stiffly. 'That won't be necessary.'

'Cristina, your father's dying.' He moved towards her. 'Right now nothing matters more than you seeing him.'

'I'm not going to see him.'

She couldn't look at him any more.

'Cristina.'

His voice was so gentle. Too gentle. It was making the ice in her heart melt.

'It's okay, *cariño*, I understand. You're in shock…you're not thinking.'

He reached out to her but she batted his hand away.

'No, you *don't* understand.'

She was almost shouting, and her body was shaking not with anger but despair—for his good opinion mattered to her, and whatever she said or did now he was going to end up thinking badly of her.

'How could you? Your parents adore you. They are so happy just to be with you. I'm nothing to my father.'

Luis flinched inwardly. He couldn't understand how this beautiful, vibrant woman should think something like that, and yet he could hear the lost note in her voice, could feel it piercing his heart.

'You're his daughter.'

She shook her head. 'I'm his dirty little secret.'

Her mouth twisted. 'Laura's his real daughter. Her mother is his wife, and she always has been his wife—even when he decided to marry my mum.' Her hand balled against her chest. 'That makes him a bigamist and me illegitimate.'

Illegitimate and therefore grotesque to a man like Luis Osorio. A man whose ties to his family were sacrosanct. A man who could trace his family back hundreds of years. He even had a castle—and a crest.

Luis took a deep breath. The pain in her eyes was like a band around his chest, and automatically he reached for her. She tried to back away but he gripped her shoulders and held her still.

'So what? I don't care.'

Her eyes widened with shock but, ignoring the expression of blatant disbelief on her face, he pulled her closer.

'Half the thrones of Europe have been filled by illegitimate children. My family's just the same.'

Thinking back to her childhood, she bit her lip. 'Your family is not the same as mine, Luis. My father led a double life for fifteen years. He lied to my mum, and to me, and when we found out, he just left us. He just disappeared. It was like he'd never existed. But then I suppose he hadn't really.'

Looking up, her mouth twisted.

'I know what you're thinking. You think there must have been some signs. But there weren't.

We were just really naive, and he was a very convincing liar.'

He held her gaze. What he'd actually been thinking was that now he understood why Cristina had reacted so strongly to finding out he was heir to the Osorio fortune. Given her father's deceit, it was hardly surprising that she had been so suspicious and distrustful of him—a man who appeared to live two very different lives.

'How did you find out?' he asked gently.

He felt her shoulders stiffen. 'He went to the airport and left his suitcase in a taxi. The driver dropped it back at our house, and when my mum unpacked it she found a letter to his accountant about a trust fund for his wife and daughter.'

Her face was rigid.

'Only it wasn't me and my mum. It was Laura and her mother. There was a photo of them too. When he rang, my mum tried to talk to him but he just hung up.'

'Did he never try to contact you?'

She shook her head. 'I found out later that he'd moved to New York. I did see him once, though.' She hesitated. 'About a year after he left. He came to London with his family. His *real* family, I mean. I'd been stalking Laura on the internet and she was all excited about the trip. I spoke to his secretary. Pretended I was Laura. She gave me the address of the hotel where he was staying and I went there.'

Her mouth dipped at the corners.

'He didn't even want to acknowledge me at first. And then, when I wouldn't leave, he pulled out his wallet and gave me a bunch of money. I threw it in his face.'

Luis squeezed her shoulders. Her voice was so steady, so matter-of-fact, but somehow that made everything worse. 'He got off easy.' It was a poor joke, but he had to say something to ease the pain in her eyes.

Cristina looked up at him, and tried, and failed to smile. 'He's my dad.'

He pulled her into his arms and suddenly it felt like the easiest, most natural thing in the world to bury her face against his chest.

'I'm sorry,' she mumbled. 'For lying to you about the phone calls. Especially after what you told me about that reporter.'

He closed his eyes 'I'm sorry too—for accusing you of all those terrible things.'

She felt his arms tighten around her.

'So what happens next? Are you just going to ignore what Laura told you?'

Lifting her face, she looked up at him, confused. 'I don't know—' she began.

But he just carried on talking as though she

hadn't spoken. 'I suppose the easiest solution is just to pretend it never happened but...'

Her eyes narrowed. 'Nice try! But I'm not going to see him. I don't want to.'

'And I understand that. But I think you *should* go—no, hear me out,' he said as she started to shake her head. 'You told me that nothing can change the past, and you were right. But you also told me that letting the past ruin your future is wrong. So go and see him and free yourself. Otherwise you'll put your life on hold forever just like I did.'

Her hands squeezed the fabric of his shirt. 'I don't think I can face him. Not on my own.'

'You won't be on your own.'

'But I can't ask my mother—'

Tipping her head back, he kissed her forehead gently. 'You won't have to. I'll be there.'

She stiffened. 'I can't ask you to do that.'

He smiled. 'You're not asking me. I'm telling you that's what's happening.'

'But why would you do that?'

Heart thumping, Luis gazed down at her. Had she guessed? Could she possibly feel the same way?

For perhaps a fraction of a second he thought about answering her truthfully. Telling her that he couldn't bear the idea of her not being there, and that he wanted to be there for her when she met her estranged father.

That in fact he wanted to be there for her always.

But, looking into her eyes, he knew it was not the right time. She needed his support—not some out-of-the-blue emotional outburst that he couldn't really explain to himself let alone her.

He shrugged. 'I pushed you into telling me about your father. That makes me kind of responsible.'

'For me?'

Cristina gazed up at him. For so long she'd had to be tough, to fight for what she wanted, and now here was Luis, offering to go into battle with her like some fairy-tale prince.

He tucked a stray strand of hair behind her ear. 'For what happens next. Now, I think we should go back to the house. You need to pack, and I need to tell Tomas to get the helicopter ready.'

As they walked back up to the house she felt dazed. She couldn't stop thinking about the look in his eyes as he'd offered to come with her. He had seemed so serious, so intense—it had felt almost as though he was offering her something else…something more than just sex.

Her breath caught.

Like a future together.

For a moment she thought about what that

would mean. What it would feel like to have a place in Luis's life and in his heart.

Her pulse stalled. It would be incredible. He was smart and sexy and sensitive, and she liked him. She liked him a lot. And it seemed like a harsh twist of fate that at the very moment she realised that fact there was no time to think, let alone act on it.

But after so many years of waiting and hoping, and pretending that she didn't care one way or another, her father finally wanted to see her—and right now that came first.

CHAPTER NINE

'WOULD YOU LIKE to go round the block one more time?'

Looking up at Luis, Cristina felt her heart thump inside her chest.

Laura had emailed her the address of the private hospital where her father was staying, and up until the moment the limousine had pulled up in a side street she had thought she was making the right decision.

But now even just looking at the gated entrance to the Hospital Virgen de la Luz in Madrid was making her throat constrict, and the palms of her hands felt damp against the leather of the bag she was clutching in her lap.

'It's okay,' Luis said, his voice gentle. 'I can text Laura…tell her we're going to be a little late—'

'No.' She shook her head. 'I've already messed her around enough. All those days of not picking up the phone—'

'Come here.' He curved his arm around her waist and pulled her against the hard muscles of his chest. 'You haven't messed anyone around.

And another couple of minutes isn't going to make much difference.'

The tension eased from her face.

'That's not what you said this morning,' she said softly.

Her expression was innocent but her eyes were anything but, and desire rose inside him, swift and strong, his body hardening faster than quick-dry cement as he remembered how he'd pressed her against him in the shower.

Lifting her chin with his hand, he held her gaze. 'Are you accusing me of being inconsistent?'

'I think insatiable might be a better fit.'

He grinned, and Cristina shook her head, but she was smiling too. How could she not? He was just so gorgeously handsome and sexy. She liked it that he was wearing a polo shirt again—this time it was grey, perhaps a shade darker than his eyes. Liked, too, the way it clung to the hard definition of his muscles.

But now was not the right time to be giving in to the heat pooling inside her. Laura and her estranged father must take priority now.

Her pulse jumped and a flurry of fear spiralled up inside of her. Was she doing the right thing?

'Yes, you are.'

She looked up at him, startled.

'No, I can't read minds. But I'd have to be completely devoid of feeling not to guess that you're nervous about this.'

And then before she could respond he bent his head and kissed her, and kept on kissing her until his lips had blotted out the fear and the doubt inside her.

As he lifted his mouth she breathed out slowly. 'Was that for luck?'

He shook his head. 'No. I'm just insatiable, remember?' Leaning forward, he tapped on the glass behind the driver's head 'You, however, are the smartest, sexiest and strongest woman I've ever met. So come on—let's go and introduce you to the other side of your family.'

As it turned out, even before Laura tentatively stepped forward to greet her, Cristina was surprised to find that meeting the woman she'd alternately envied and despised for so many years was easier than she'd anticipated.

In fact, although both women were clearly on edge, their main reaction to one another seemed to be not resentment and hostility but surprise.

Maybe that was down to the fact that they were alike in so many ways. Weirdly alike. Same height, same eyes, same way of standing with one foot turned out.

It was still awkward, of course—how could it not be? And perhaps if Luis hadn't been there they might have carried on making polite but wooden conversation about Laura's hotel and Cristina's journey. But something in his quiet, calm manner seemed to ease the tension between them, so that both she and Laura began to relax, and the three of them spoke easily for five minutes or so before Laura offered to find a nurse and tell her that Cristina had arrived.

While she was gone, Luis pulled her close. 'You two seem to be getting along okay.'

Cristina nodded. Her skin felt too tight, and she didn't seem to be able to breathe properly.

'I didn't think I'd like her,' she said shakily. 'Or that she'd like me. I was just so hung up on the fact that we were only half-sisters.'

He drew a finger over her cheek. 'Two halves make a whole.'

Her mouth trembled, but when she looked up at him, his eyes calmed her.

'It's going to be all right.'

'Is it?'

He nodded automatically, but as she looked up at him the expression on her face stayed his heart. 'Your father has asked to see you, *carino*. Let's just start with that.'

'Cristina!'

It was Laura. Beside her stood a young woman dressed in a pale blue tunic and trousers.

'We can go in now.'

The short walk to her father's private room seemed to take for ever. Her heart was beating painfully fast, and if it hadn't been for Luis's hand firmly gripping hers she might well have turned and run.

But in him there was something reassuringly solid—not just in his grip but in his manner. It was nothing overt. On the contrary, he was quiet and courteous. There was, though, a subtle natural authority about him that seemed to resonate with those around him.

Watching the busy hospital come to a virtual standstill, she felt warmth swell in her chest. She had never imagined trusting a man—and right now she had never felt more vulnerable—and yet with Luis by her side she felt safe in a way that she'd craved since her father had ripped any ability to trust away from her at the age of thirteen.

And now she was going to see him for the first time in eleven years…maybe for the last time.

She hadn't seen him since that terrible scene in the hotel. Enrique Lastra had been stocky then, with a broad, square head like a bull and mass of thick black hair that had earned him his nickname—Mino, from *minotauro*, the half-man, half-bull of Greek mythology.

But there was nothing imposing about the man in the hospital bed.

True, he had that same mass of hair. Only now

it was almost white. An ache was building in her chest and she stared at him dazedly, barely registering Laura's hand on her arm as her sister pulled her towards the bed.

'*Holà*, Papá. It's me… Laura.'

Cristina felt her stomach clench as her father's eyes opened, for they hadn't changed. They were still the same dark brown she remembered, and that only seemed to make her chest ache even more. His eyes might not have changed but everything else had—not just his appearance but in their relationship too.

'Laura…' His voice hadn't changed either. It was still a distinctive rasp—the legacy of a life spent smoking, first cigarettes and then later cigars.

She watched as her half-sister smiled. 'I'm here, Papá, and I've got someone here with me. Someone I know you want to see.'

Cristina's pulse rippled as her father turned his head slowly towards her. But if she'd been expecting a tearful gasp of recognition she was to be disappointed.

Enrique stared at her blankly. 'I don't—'

'It's Cristina, Papá,' Laura said quickly. 'She's come to see you.'

His eyes narrowed then, and Cristina waited for him to acknowledge her, but instead he turned back to Laura.

'What does *she* want?'

Laura glanced over at her but Cristina said nothing.

It was clear from her sister's stricken face that Enrique had not wanted to see her at all. Probably it had been Laura's idea—a misguided desire to reunite her dying father with his estranged daughter—but they both knew without having to say it out loud that he had nothing to say to her.

If only that she could tell him that she didn't want anything from him, and that he was as big a disappointment to her as she had obviously been to him. But the words stuck in her throat, and she was scared that if she pushed them out then the tears she was also holding back might burst free too.

She couldn't see Luis's face, but she felt his hand tighten around hers, could feel the hard breadth of his chest at her shoulder, and more than anything she wanted to turn and bury her head against it. But to do that would mean showing how hurt she was.

How hurt and humiliated.

Biting down on the howl of anguish filling her lungs, she turned and walked swiftly towards the door, just as a nurse pushed a trolley through it. Sidestepping it, she heard Luis curse and Laura call out her name, and then she was running through the corridors and down the stairs, out into the street and then into another street, and then another, tears streaming down her face.

Finally she could run no more and, whimpering, she crouched down in a doorway like a wounded animal and cried—just as she'd cried eleven years ago when she'd realised that her father wasn't coming back and that he didn't want or love her.

Striding into the living room of his family's apartment on the exclusive Calle de Velázquez, Luis tugged off his jacket and punched Cristina's number into his phone for perhaps the twentieth time. His mouth tightened as it went straight to voicemail again and he didn't leave a message. There was no point. He'd already left a whole bunch of messages and she hadn't responded to any of them.

Where *was* she? More importantly, was she okay?

Remembering the look of devastation on her face as she'd left her father's room, he felt a rush of anger towards the man lying in the bed.

How could anyone be so cruel as to turn away from their own child?

His heart was pounding in time with his headache. It was nearly two hours since she'd fled from the hospital. In between calling her phone he'd tried to find her, stopping in bars and cafés, convinced that he would somehow catch sight of her just as he had that first night.

But he hadn't and so, knowing that sooner or later she'd have to go back to the apartment, he'd decided to wait for her there.

Too impatient to wait for the lift, he'd taken the stairs three at a time, and as he'd walked in he'd half hoped she might have returned. But she wasn't waiting for him in the living room, or the bedroom. Nor had Elena, the housekeeper, seen her. Everywhere was silent and empty.

It was a silence that reminded him painfully of his family home in the days and weeks following his brother's death and, suddenly unable to bear the memories of that time, he reached for his jacket. He couldn't just stand here doing nothing.

His heart jolted in his chest as somewhere in the building he heard a door close.

'Cristina?'

He was halfway across the floor when she walked into the room.

'*Cariño*. Thank goodness.' Pulse racing, he pulled her against him, touching her hair with his lips, feeling her exhaustion.'

As his arms tightened around her Cristina leaned into his chest, the scent of his cologne and the warmth of his body enveloping her. It would be so easy just to stay there for ever in an eternal embrace…

But he was not hers to hold.

Breathing out slowly, she shifted backwards.

His arms loosened, and as she looked up at him he said, 'I went looking for you and I tried calling—'

His voice was steady but she could feel his pulse leaping beneath his skin. He had been *worried* about her, and the fact that he cared made her want to cry all over again.

But instead she managed a weak smile. 'I put my phone on silent when we went into the hospital...' Her voice faltered. Her skin felt numb and her brain seemed to be working at half-speed, but she could picture it still—her father's face as he'd turned and looked at her. Or rather looked through her. As though she wasn't there. As though she didn't matter.

Her stomach gave a lurch.

She had gone to see him, believing that he wanted to see her. That he wanted to talk to her, make amends, maybe even ask for forgiveness.

Forgiveness? What a joke!

Suddenly she was perilously close to tears again.

He hadn't even known she was coming, and he certainly hadn't wanted to see or speak to her, much less ask for forgiveness. Nothing had changed. He still didn't love her or want anything to do with her.

An ache of misery was spreading inside her. It had been crushing to realise that fact when she was thirteen. More crushing still a year later, when he'd turned his back on her in that hotel foyer, for that time his rejection had been public.

But at least then her pain and shame had only been witnessed by strangers. This time Laura and Luis had been there to see that she was not worthy of love—not even from her own father.

'Cristina?'

She felt Luis's fingers curl around her hand.

'You have every right to be upset. But your father's very ill. He didn't know what he was saying.'

She shrugged. 'I know that, and I'm fine. Really, it doesn't matter.'

Like hell it didn't.

To Luis, the aftershocks from that encounter with her father were palpable. Her face was pale and set, and she had obviously been crying, His stomach muscles clenched and he felt anger spike inside him for he hated seeing her so upset.

But he was just going to have to keep his feelings under wraps. Right now, Cristina came first.

Realising that he needed to tread carefully, he glanced at his watch. 'Look, it's nearly three o'clock Let's have something to eat now, and then maybe we can pop back to the hospital tomorrow—'

Her head snapped up.

'Or we could go back today,' he said.

Slowly she shook her head. 'I'm not going back today or tomorrow or any other day. Don't you understand, Luis? I don't want to see my father again. Not now. Not ever.'

He held up his hands placatingly. 'I know you feel that now, but—'

'But what?' Cristina looked up at him challengingly. 'Do you seriously think it will make any difference how many times I go back to that hospital? You saw him today—he didn't even want to look at me.'

'I know. But he was probably in shock. He wasn't expecting to see you—'

'So what are you saying? That this is *my* fault, somehow?'

He frowned. 'No, of course not. I just meant that he'll have had a bit of time to think—'

She cut him off before he had a chance to finish his sentence. '*A bit of time?* How much does he need? He's had eleven years.'

She shook her head. She was breathing too fast and the ache inside her chest was building.

'You just don't get it, do you? I could wait *one hundred* years and it wouldn't change the way he feels about me.'

'You don't know that,' Luis said quietly. 'You came here to face your past, Cristina, not to run away from it.'

She threw his hand off hers, her eyes blazing with anger and hurt. 'How dare you?'

Her words were barely above a whisper, but he could feel the force of them as though she were shouting.

'I was upset—'

'And you were right to be.' Reaching out, he grasped her hands in his. 'Totally and justifiably right. But that doesn't change the fact that if you walk away now all this will have been for nothing.'

He took a step towards her, keeping his grey gaze steady on her face.

'I know you don't want to hear it, but trust me, *cariño*. You can't run away from this. I know because I tried.'

She stared at him mutely, the truth of his words silencing her. He was right, but knowing that didn't seem to make any difference. She still felt sick with fear.

Trust me. It was so easy for him to say, but a virtual impossibility for her to do. She had loved her father, trusted him unconditionally. He had helped her with her homework, dug sandcastles with her on the beach, taught her to ride a bike, and none of it had mattered. When it came to it he had simply turned his back on her.

Her body began to tremble. The first time she had been a child. It had been out of her control, and the same had been true about their meeting at the hotel. But what had happened today at the hospital was different. *She* was different—older and in control of her life. She was an adult now, and if she let this happen again—if she let him reject her again—then it would not be bad luck, or a mistake. It would be a choice.

A choice she was *not* willing to make.

'I know you're trying to help, but it's not the same,' she said flatly. 'You and I are not the same.'

Her heart began to beat faster as she remembered how she had allowed herself to imagine being not just in Luis's bed but in his life. Maybe if Luis had been a different man from a different background, and they had met under different circumstances, she might have let herself be swept away by his tenderness and support, given in to some kind of romantic fantasy.

But there was no point in reading anything into his gesture. Luis might be loyal and strong and handsome like a prince, but he was also wealthy like a prince too. Wealthy, privileged, and with all the expectations of his birth.

Her mouth tightened. Expectations that would never include her. This wouldn't last. It couldn't. Not just because they came from opposite ends of the social spectrum, or even because she was illegitimate. It had to do with her, and what she knew deep down to be true and immutable about herself.

That beneath all her bravado she was a let-down.

'I'm not going back to see my father. There's no point. I'm done with that part of my life now. It's time to move on and...' She hesitated, but only for a moment. 'And I'm not going back to the island with you either.'

It had been hard enough saying the words inside her head. Speaking them out loud made her stomach turn inside out with misery. But that was nothing to the pain she would feel if she went back with him and waited for him to end it—as he surely would.

Luis stared at her in shock, his hands tightening on hers involuntarily. She had stilled, her body tensing, and he could sense that already she was retreating—just as she had before.

The breath in his throat felt thick and cloying, and panic rose up inside him as he imagined the island without her—his life without her.

He'd seen the doubt and fear in her eyes when he'd asked her to trust him, and he knew that he needed to do something, say something to calm her, to stop her closing off and withdrawing from him. To make her trust him.

'I know how much your father's hurt you, Cristina. He's hurt you and that's why you don't want to go and see him again. You don't trust him not to hurt you more.'

He paused, the doubt and fear on her face staying his words for a moment, and then he breathed out slowly.

'I know you don't trust me either, and you think I'm going to hurt you too. But I could never hurt you, *cariño*.' Heart thumping, he held her gaze. 'I love you, Cristina.'

Her brows drew together and she looked up at him uncertainly.

It wasn't that he was lying. She knew with absolute certainty that he believed what he was saying. Just as her father had believed it when he'd stood in front of a room full of witnesses and told her mother that he'd love and cherish her for ever.

But the problem was that she didn't believe it.

Worse, she knew how it would play out, for she'd been in this exact place before, with previous boyfriends. Only she had never felt like this before, and that was what was scaring her the most.

She already cared far too much about Luis. Soon she'd panic like she always did, about losing her place in his affections and then it would just be a matter of time before he realised that she wasn't worthy of his love, his time or his attention.

Better to get out now, with her dignity and her heart intact.

Gently, she slid her hands from beneath his. 'One day you are going to find thewoman who will make you happy.'

There was a long, loaded silence. He stared at her, a flicker of confusion in his eyes, as though he hadn't quite understood what she had said—as though she had spoken in a foreign language.

'I have found her,' he said finally.

She shook her head. 'I like you, Luis, and I'm grateful—'

'Grateful!'

The word sounded harsh as it echoed around the beautiful room.

'Yes, for everything you've done, for your help and support. But that's all I feel.' She clenched her jaw, biting down on the lie. 'We said we didn't want anything serious. Don't you remember?'

She watched his face shift and harden as anger replaced confusion.

'Yes, I remember. But that was before all this.'

'This doesn't change anything.' She spoke quickly, for with every passing second it was getting harder to believe that leaving Luis was the right thing to do. 'I'm sorry if you thought it did, but it doesn't. My life is a big enough mess right now—I don't need or want any more complications.'

'And that's what I am, is it?'

His voice was steady, but the expression on his face made her want to curl up somewhere dark and private.

'A complication?'

Luis stared at her in silence. His head was spinning; anger and misery were rippling through him in waves, tangling up with his breath so that his chest felt full of knots. He knew she was scared of being hurt, and that she found it hard to trust. So he'd offered himself and his feelings up like a sacrifice to prove that he could be trusted.

He'd thought it would be enough.

But he'd been wrong.

Trust wasn't the issue. She just didn't want him.

For her this had only ever been a fling. A short-term sexual liaison.

His anguish felt like a living thing.

Not just because he was losing her but because he saw now that he'd never really had her.

Something seemed to fall forward high up inside him.

He'd fallen in love and he'd wanted her to feel the same way—so much so that he'd trusted his emotions over the evidence, put feelings before facts. It was the emotional equivalent of a HALO jump without a parachute. The ultimate gamble.

And he'd lost.

He hadn't heard her leave the room but she must have done, for suddenly she was standing there with her bag.

'I'm going to stay in a hotel.'

'There's no need,' he said flatly. 'There's no reason for me to stay now, so you might as well use the apartment.'

Cristina shook her head. Her body was so rigid with misery that it hurt to make that tiny sideways movement, but she didn't care. In fact she was grateful, for it gave her something to concentrate on aside from the crack opening up inside her heart.

'Thank you, but no. I'd rather stay at a hotel.' She hesitated. 'I'll write to your parents.'

He nodded. 'What about your things? On the island?'

She shrugged. 'Throw them away. I have everything I want.'

It was a lie. The thought of walking away, of leaving Luis behind for ever, was like staring into a star as it exploded. She knew that afterwards she would be left blind and broken, but there was no alternative—or none that she could imagine. It was like trying to picture what lay beyond the horizon.

To stay would only prolong the agony.

There was nothing left to say.

As she lifted her bag and walked towards the

door Luis watched, his body frozen, his brain silently pleading with her to stop and turn around. His heart aching for her to change her mind.

But she didn't so much as hesitate, and he was still standing there when he heard the door close behind her and felt the silence of the empty apartment rise up around him.

CHAPTER TEN

SCOOPING HER HAIR up into a ponytail-cum-bun, Cristina sat down on the bed in her Madrid hotel room and breathed out slowly, trying to control the irregular beat of her heart as she looked down at her phone.

She scrolled slowly through the messages and missed calls. She'd already checked twice that morning, and she knew—*knew*—that there was no point, but she couldn't stop herself from doing it.

Just in case by some miracle Luis had texted or called her.

Don't cry, she told herself. *You promised that today you wouldn't cry.*

She blinked furiously.

Switching off her phone, she swallowed past the lump of misery wedged in her throat. It had been the same every day since she'd walked out of the Osorios' apartment. No text, no message. Nothing.

That had been a month ago.

A month spent trying not to think about Luis.

Trying and *failing* not to think about Luis.

Her chest felt heavy and tight. Even now she

could remember that look on his face as she'd left, his hurt and confusion as he'd tried to hold himself together.

Suddenly she was fighting to catch her breath, fighting not to give in to the tears that had fallen ceaselessly since that last day with him. She'd even woken at night and found her face wet and her pillow damp.

She had never felt more miserable and desperate, and the fact that her misery was self-imposed was no consolation at all. Life—hers and other people's—had just stopped mattering, and she wanted to do nothing but lie in bed in her pyjamas with the curtains drawn.

It was Laura who had helped her. Her half-sister and now her friend. It had been Laura who had booked her into the same hotel as her. Laura who had fed her and forced her to get dressed, listened to her talk and cry—sometimes both at the same time.

She breathed in shakily. At least she had been able to support her half-sister when their father had died quietly in his sleep ten days ago. It was the main reason she had chosen to stay in Spain. And even though she hadn't gone back to see Enrique again Laura had understood. Just as she had understood Laura's need to be by his bedside.

Since his death Laura had been tied up with arrangements for the funeral, but they met for breakfast or lunch most days, and supper every evening, and Laura had already begged Cristina to come and stay with her in America.

America.

She stared lethargically across the room. Six weeks ago she would have killed to do something as glamorous and exciting as go to New York. And she was excited about going, but also a little nervous too—for Laura wanted to introduce her to her mother, Nina, the woman who had been her father's wife and then ex-wife.

Cristina had been shocked to learn that Nina and Enrique had been divorced for seven years. Shocked too by how that made her feel. Given everything that had happened with her father, it would have been logical and completely understandable for her to feel that he'd got his comeuppance. Instead, though, she simply felt sad.

But it was a sadness that she could contain, for Enrique had been absent from her for so long that it felt as though she'd already spent almost half her life grieving for him.

In contrast, Luis's absence felt like a raw wound, an ache that would never heal. How could it? He had been a part of her, and without him she would never feel whole again.

She felt the sting of tears and, brushing at her eyes, stood up quickly and looked round for her handbag. As she did so she caught sight of her reflection in one of the gilt-framed mirrors on the wall and, pausing, reached up and touched her hair.

It had been auburn for so many years but now it was what her mother called 'mouse'.

She looked familiar, yet different. It was like meeting someone from the past, and in a way she was. 'Mouse' had been her father's nickname for her, and that had been one of the reasons she had decided to dye her hair in the first place. It had been a teenager's angry response to being forgotten—a way of standing out and mattering.

It had taken a long time, but it had worked.

Grace had been delighted with her photos of Agusto and Sofia. So delighted that she had instantly commissioned Cristina to do an interview with an award-winning *madrileño* actor, and to shoot the French-born striker who had just won his third Golden Boot trophy for a cover.

But despite earning herself a permanent position at the magazine, and loving spending time with Laura, she still felt listless—numb, almost.

And lonely.

Her throat tightened. All her life she had been chasing a dream. A dream of being accepted. Of belonging. But now that her dream was a reality she realised that it wasn't enough. That there was only one person whose acceptance she craved. Only one person to whom she truly wanted to belong.

Only he wasn't here. She had pushed him away and then walked away from him. And now she would never see Luis again.

She breathed in, consciously refusing to let her thoughts spiral down again. It was done, and she'd had no choice. Letting Luis get close to her was too big a risk to take.

All she could do now was focus on the positive—her job and her sister.

Her sister! Glancing at her phone, she swore softly.

The sister she was supposed to be meeting for lunch in fifteen minutes.

If she left now, she thought, she might just get there on time. And, snatching up her bag and room key, she ran towards the door.

She was hot and sticky by the time she arrived at the café.

'Sorry,' she said, throwing her bag down onto the spare chair and then kissing Laura on both cheeks. 'I completely forgot the time.'

Her sister rolled her eyes. 'It's fine. I only just got here myself.' Leaning back, she squinted up at the sun. 'I thought we had long meetings at the museum, but I honestly thought the one I had this morning would never end.'

Cristina felt a pang of guilt. Following Enrique's death, Laura had been saddled with meeting the various lawyers and bankers that her father had employed to manage his business affairs.

She frowned. 'Can I do anything? Oh, thank you.' She glanced up as the waiter put two bottles of water, some bread and olives on the table. 'I know I've been pretty useless lately, but I want to help.'

Tearing at a piece of bread, Laura shook her head. 'I know you do. But I'm just whining, really.' She glanced at the menu. 'Is there anything you particularly want? Or shall I just order for us both?'

Cristina glanced inside the café to the counter, where dark grey slates were piled up high with grilled chorizo and white asparagus wrapped in Riojan cheese.

'No, you choose. But be quick.' She grinned at her sister. 'I'm starving.'

The *tapas* arrived before they'd finished the bread. They were hot and moreish and full of smoky flavour.

As the waiter arranged the small terracotta dishes efficiently over every available space on the small table she felt her mouth start to tingle. Despite the family atmosphere of the café, some of the *tapas* were so beautiful they looked like canapés at some upmarket party, or starters from a Michelin-starred restaurant.

Her fingers tightened around her fork.

Damn. She had promised herself that she wouldn't think about Luis over lunch, but her brain had made the leap from Michelin-starred restaurant to that meal with his parents with astonishing speed.

'Are you okay?' Laura was looking at her anxiously. 'Did you burn yourself?'

Cristina shook her head. 'No, I was just thinking—'

'About Luis.' Her half-sister finished the sentence for her.

'Not really—' Catching sight of Laura's expression of disbelief, she sighed. 'Well, okay—yes, I was. But it has been at least three minutes,' she joked weakly. 'And, on the plus side, I haven't cried at all today.'

Reaching across the table, Laura squeezed her sister's arm reassuringly.

'I'm fine—honestly. And if eat everything on this table I'll be in so much pain I won't be able move, let alone cry. So pass me the *alcachofas*... and I'll have some of that *mojama* too.'

Looking over at Laura, she felt her smile fade from her face. She had expected to see her sister smiling back at her, but instead Laura was gripping the edge of the table, and her light brown eyes were watching Cristina with a mixture of uncertainty and fear.

'What is it? Has something happened?' She

felt a rush of panic and remorse. Laura was always so calm, so steady. 'Did something happen at your meeting?'

Her sister shook her head. 'It's nothing to do with the meeting or with me.' She hesitated. 'It's about you. Only—'

'Only what?' Cristina breathed in sharply, trying to shift the knot of fear lodged in her chest as her sister's fingers clenched and unclenched against the table.

'I want to tell you, only I'm worried it's going to upset you—'

'What are you talking about?' she said hoarsely.

There was a short, tense silence, and then Laura reached into her bag and pulled out an envelope. Cristina felt her mouth turn dry as she spotted the familiar crest above Laura's name and the address of their hotel.

She stared at it numbly as Laura cleared her throat.

'It's from Luis. It came a couple of days ago.' She bit her lip. 'I know I should have given it to you right away, Chrissie, but you've been so upset. And then, when you started to seem a bit happier, I didn't want to make it worse again.'

Looking up into her sister's anguished face, Cristina drew in another breath, still trying to stay calm.

'Why did he write to you?'

Laura held her gaze steadily, but when she spoke there was a quiver to her voice.

'He came to the hospital the day after…you know…' A flush of colour spread over her cheeks. 'After you left him. He asked to see Papá alone.'

'Why? What for?' Now it was Cristina's cheeks that were burning.

'Just read the letter, Chrissie. Then you'll know why.'

Laura held out the envelope, and after a moment or two Cristina took it.

She stared at the cursive handwriting on the front, watching the letters slip in and out of focus, and then with hands that were surprisingly steady she pulled out the letter and read it.

Dear Laura,
I was so saddened to hear about the death of your father. Please accept my condolences. I know from the short time of seeing the two of you together that you were close, and that he loved you very much. But you don't need me to tell you that. You were at the heart of your father's life.

Sadly, however, the same was not true for Cristina.

She believes that she meant nothing to her father, and that she had nothing in common with Enrique.

But she is wrong on both counts.

When I spoke to him at the hospital I discovered that he was just as proud and stubborn as she is.

He told me that he regretted not speaking to Cristina when she visited him. That he had always loved her and wanted to reach out to her but was too scared of being judged for the actions he had always regretted but never had the courage to face.

He also told me how very proud he was of Cristina—not just her career but her courage—and that had he been brave enough to do so he would have been proud to call her his daughter.

Unfortunately, as we both know, Cristina did not get a chance to learn of Enrique's true feelings for her. Nor would she believe me if I told her. I feel, though, that she would believe you. I therefore ask if you would share this letter with her so that maybe, finally, she can believe in herself.

Please take care of her for me.
Yours sincerely,
Luis

The words were swirling in front of her eyes. She knew that Luis loved her. He had told her so. But what she hadn't realised until now was that she loved him too. Loved him so much that her heart felt as though it would burst.

'Oh, Laura.' She looked up, tears spilling over her cheeks. 'What have I done? What have I *done*?'

Stopping at the edge of the cliff, Luis gazed out towards the horizon. The sun had already burned away the early-morning haze of cloud and was now shimmering like a huge golden orb in the sky. Past the dark grey rocks, white-topped waves were slicing through the smooth blue surface of the water. It was going to be a glorious day.

He glanced at the sea longingly. Maybe next time he would take the boat out—right now, though, he wanted to go swimming.

Stepping back, he made his way down the cliff path towards the tidal pool. The beach was his usual destination for an early-morning swim, but he was feeling lazy today. Today he simply wanted to enjoy the delicious and still novel feeling of playing truant in the sunshine. And what better way to do that than by lying on his back and gazing up at this cloudless sky, buoyed up by the warm Mediterranean water?

The last four weeks had been some of the busiest and most chaotic in his life. Having decided to move back to Spain permanently, he had finally sat down with his father and the lawyers yesterday and formally taken over as chairman of Banco Osorio. And last week he'd flown back to California to sort out his business affairs and arrange the sale of his properties.

Returning to Segovia, he'd known immediately that he'd made the right decision. Even without his parents' joy it had felt as if he was coming home.

But, although he was happy to be back, he felt Cristina's absence every minute of every hour. At times he thought he was losing his mind with the misery of losing her. Just like with Bas, he felt as if a part of him was missing—almost as though when she'd walked away she'd taken something with her.

His legs slowed to a halt and, closing his eyes, he let the pain wash over him.

That was why he'd returned to the island alone. To face the pain head-on in the place where he and Cristina had become lovers.

He might have met her in that club in Segovia, but that night had been about sex and oblivion.

This was where the miracle had happened— where the barriers he'd built between himself and the world had started to crumble. And this was where he needed to be to start the long process of rebuilding his life.

Without her.

Opening his eyes, he breathed out slowly. Cristina was gone from his life, and only by exorcising the memory of her and his hopes for what might have been could he hope to move on.

The ache inside his chest was suddenly so big that he thought it might break through his skin. He didn't *want* to move on. He wanted to go back in time—go back to the moment when she'd needed him.

Except that wouldn't work, for even if he could stop time it wouldn't change the eventual outcome. Cristina didn't love him, and however painful it was to accept that fact he needed to do it.

Bas's death had taught him that.

Life was for living, not for grieving.

But he did just want one last moment before he reset the clock for ever...

From somewhere nearby he heard a splash, and the sound pulled him back to the present. Theoretically he could stay here for as long as he wanted, but he'd made a deal with himself. One last swim and then he would go home.

Turning towards the oval of clear blue water set into the rocks, he made his way across the warm limestone slabs—and abruptly stopped.

A woman was swimming smoothly beneath the water.

He couldn't see her face, but then he didn't need to. Even with the sun glaring off the water, dazzling his eyes, the curve of her back was unmistakable. Unforgettable.

Staring down at her, he felt his stomach seem to go into free fall, just as though he'd dived off the rock to join her. He watched, dry-mouthed, as she slow-crawled to the side and pulled herself up onto one of the flat plateaux that edged the pool, blinking water out of her eyes, leaving her hair—*her brown hair*—clinging to the contours of her skull.

Cristina.

He forced himself to say her name inside his head, and just as though she'd heard him she turned and their eyes met.

For the longest moment neither of them moved. They just gazed at one another. And then suddenly she was walking towards him.

His skin was prickling with shock.

It must be a dream. Or some kind of optical illusion. Maybe he was hallucinating...

He stared at her in silence as she picked her way across the rocks, his breath catching fire in his throat as she stopped in front him.

Since she'd walked out of his life he'd thought about her endlessly, replayed every glance, every word they'd shared, imagined whole conversations inside his head, and he knew that he should say something—that he *needed* to say something. Yet now she was here both his mouth and his brain seemed to have stopped working.

But as he looked down into her face it suddenly

didn't matter what he said, for he could see her tears mingling with the drops of seawater and he knew that no words were needed.

Her heart belonged to him just as his heart belonged to her.

And, reaching out, he tugged her to him, an ache of love and longing swelling inside his chest.

'You came back,' he said softly, fighting back his own tears. He felt her nod against him. 'But how did you know I was here?'

Cristina swallowed. 'I spoke to your father.'

'My *father*?'

She almost laughed at the shock in his voice.

'He was so sweet. And kind.'

'He likes you.'

She felt Luis's lips brush against her hair.

'And I like him. But I like you more—so very much more.'

His heart gave a thump as she tilted her head back and he saw that fresh tears were sliding over her cheeks.

'I love you, Luis. I have done for ages, only I was too scared to let myself feel it. And then, when you told me that you loved me, I was too scared to trust you. I just couldn't believe I could have a place in your life.

'So what changed?' he asked shakily.

She smiled weakly. 'I realised that you *are* my life.'

Her eyes were soft and unwavering.

'I've missed you so much. Every day I woke up thinking of something to tell you, and you weren't there. Every street I walked down I'd reach out for your hand, and you weren't there. And every night when I fell asleep I wanted to feel you next to me, but you weren't there.'

Luis could hardly breathe. She was baring her soul to him, proving not only that she loved him but that she trusted him too.

His arms tightened around her. 'I felt the same way. Nothing matters without you, Cristina. You're my life. My world. *Mi corazón.*'

And, taking her face between his hands, he kissed her fiercely.

Finally he raised his head, fixed his grey eyes on hers. 'I love you.'

Cristina felt her heart contract. He sounded so serious. So full of certainty...

She glanced up him, her lips trembling—and not only from the force of his kiss.

'Enough to marry me?' The words scrambled from her mouth before she could stop them.

He drew back, his eyes widening with shock and surprise, those beautiful grey eyes that she had missed so much searching her face.

'Are you asking me to marry you?'

Cristina held his gaze. The certainty she had

craved for her entire life rose up inside her and she nodded. 'Yes. Yes, I am.'

She held her breath, her pulse jumping with hope and love, and then with joy as relief and happiness spread across his face and he kissed her again.

'Is that a yes?' she croaked, when finally he lifted his mouth.

He pulled her closer, steadying her body against his, his eyes as dark and damp as the surf-splashed rocks beneath their feet.

'No. But *this* is.'

And, lowering his mouth, he kissed her again, pressing her so close that nothing could come between them.

* * * * *

If you enjoyed
SURRENDER TO THE
RUTHLESS BILLIONAIRE,
you'll love these other stories by Louise Fuller!

KIDNAPPED FOR THE TYCOON'S BABY
BLACKMAILED DOWN THE AISLE
CLAIMING HIS WEDDING NIGHT
A DEAL SEALED BY PASSION

Available now!